CW00377262

Ramatel's Vow

Book Two in A Series of Angels
By Joel Crofoot

Edited by Zoe Snow

Cover Art by Kristyn McQuiggan

Chapter One

Ramatel plucked his black cargo pants off the bedroom floor where he had abandoned them the night before and gave them a visual inspection for cleanliness. The pants showed no obvious signs of demonic blood or excessive dirt, so he donned them, then he added a pair of socks and black combat boots to his attire. He always dressed himself in black when he was fighting demons because it helped him hide in the shadows.

He was reaching for a shirt from a laundry basket that the staff had delivered earlier in the week when a loud, sharp crack of lightning struck behind him in the room. The room lit up, as if the sun had been brought down to earth for a brief second, and Ramatel was nearly knocked over by the force of the pressure.

Oh God! Literally, or at least it was his handiwork.

Ramatel turned around and found himself facing a small woman with pale skin and long dark, red hair. She wore the traditional garb of heaven, a white flowing linen cloth. Her wide green eyes scanned her surroundings, catching and reflecting the light like little emeralds. She seemed to be just as shocked from the blast as he was. Only angels coming from heaven ever entered a room that way. He tried to hide a snarl at the unwelcome intrusion, at least, until he could find out who she was and what she wanted.

Know your enemy.

Ramatel narrowed his eyes at her and saw that her exposed skin was covered with freckles. She was short, almost a foot shorter than he was. She wavered as if she was having trouble balancing from the transition, then her eyes locked on him.

She froze utterly still at the sight of him. With no words or explanation offered, she just stared at him like she was in a room with a cornered tiger. There was no hiding the fear in her expression, and a part of him didn't blame her.

Being topless, hundreds of scars were visible, intricately carved all over his skin, including half of his face. His black hair had regrown to cover the scars on crown of his head. But the hair had only regrown to about to the tops of his ears, so it did nothing to conceal the pink, raised skin on his neck. The design that had been carved into his face parted the hair of his eyebrows and disfigured the right half of his lips. He immediately felt the urge to turn away from this woman from the shame of his appearance. And that pissed him off. *Why should I hide from her? She is the one popping up, uninvited, in my room.*

"Who the fuck are you?" he demanded loudly, reaching for his shirt in spite of his anger.

She backed away at his sudden display of aggression. "I'm Clara," she managed, barely above a whisper.

Ramatel was pleased with her reaction. Fear meant she would steer clear of him. Steering clear meant not having to answer questions about his scars or deal with the visual scrutiny others subjected him to when they thought he wasn't looking. He pulled his shirt over his head, then advanced on her a little bit. "What do you want Clara?"

"Um, I don't know. Who are you?"

Ramatel ignored her question. He was in charge here. Not her. He'd be asking the questions. "What are you doing here?"

"Where am I? Who are you?"

Probably a brand new angel. Who is she to question me? She is the one invading my privacy, judging my skin. Fucken angelings these days, no respect!

"Who sent you?" he bit out.

She looked around his trashed room as if taking in her surroundings for the first time. Her eyes landed on a hole he had punched in the wall a few months ago. She made no comment, but his anger rose with every sight she gleaned as he imagined what she would think of his room, which was littered with broken furniture and wall holes. Even his room had scars.

She looked back at him when he took another step in her direction. She seemed to find her courage then. "All I know is that some voice said this is my chance for redemption, and the next thing I know, here I am."

"You're part of the help the Father promised?" He eyed her skeptically. *Obviously when the Father promised Gabriel help he'd meant house staff.* He was disappointed. He was hoping for more fighters. Apparently, she had landed in the wrong place. "Come with me."

Ramatel led her out of the back house of Gabriel's estate. He was grateful that his roommates were already out. He didn't feel like explaining why he had a woman in his room, especially one wearing a toga. He rolled his eyes at the thought of the ridicule he would have received.

The sun was just setting as he led her across the lawn, past the pool, toward the main house. The sound of crickets chirping filled the silence as they walked. The back door to the main house opened to the kitchen. From there he escorted her through the sitting room and up one of the staircases. He was headed to Gabriel's study. The archangel would probably still be seeing lesser angels who sought his counsel. The door to the study was closed and Ramatel could hear voices from inside so he ushered her to the waiting area.

"Sit," he commanded, pointing to a beige sofa in front of a coral colored wall. The room, like the rest of the house, was decorated like a museum of ancient artifacts. Several of the artifacts were on display in glass cases. The theme of this room was ancient religious texts. Encased within the wall on glass shelves, the remnants of historic books and scrolls were displayed.

She walked past them slowly, trying to look at each one, on her way to the couch Ramatel had pointed to. Ramatel leaned against the door jamb with his arms crossed and stared at her. She fidgeted under his gaze, and he liked that. Uncomfortability meant she wouldn't look at him. It also gave him ample opportunity to study her.

Her pink lips were the perfect shade for her pale skin, and they made the green of her eyes stand out more. Her perfectly arched eyebrows topped off light eyelashes that matched her red hair. She wasn't wearing any makeup, but she still held all the beauty that Ramatel would never know again. Not a scar to be seen. *She probably doesn't even appreciate it.*

The door to Gabriel's study opened. While saying their goodbyes, Gabriel escorted the angel he'd been talking to out into the hall. The two clasped hands and the lesser angel turned to leave. He tried to walk by Ramatel but not before Ramatel noticed the shock on the man's face when their eyes met. Ramatel glared back, daring him to look again but the man's eyes immediately diverted to the floor and he shuffled toward the stairs.

"Gabriel, we have another one," Ramatel pointed to the white clad woman in the waiting room.

"No one else was scheduled tonight," Gabriel said, his tone rank with curiosity.

"Not a visitor, help. She landed in my room."

Gabriel's eyes opened in surprise and he studied Ramatel's expression for a moment.

"Do you know what that means?" Gabriel asked.

Ramatel pinched his eyebrows together, but he didn't answer. *It means something?*

"Bring her in," Gabriel gestured to his study.

Ramatel barked at the girl to follow him again and Gabriel led them into his study. It was dark outside now so the windows behind his desk did nothing to light the room. The deficit was filled by a giant chandelier providing yellow light, augmented by several floor lamps.

Gabriel approached the woman with a gentle smile and all the congeniality that Ramatel lacked. "Pleased to meet you Miss. I'm Gabriel."

"Clara," she shook his outstretched hand.

"Please have a seat Clara. Can I get you anything?" Gabriel led her to an overstuffed chair in the sitting area in front of his massive desk. She shook her head and Ramatel turned to leave, glad his part in this was over. People made him uncomfortable, except for the other fallen and those who were there at his rising.

"Please sit, Brother," Gabriel called to him just he made it to the door.

Ramatel gave Gabriel a "What the hell," look, but he returned to the sitting area and chose a chair across from Clara, with a coffee table between them. Ramatel sat back and crossed his arms, eyeing the girl. She sat forward in her chair with a tense posture and her shoulders drawn high.

Gabriel seated himself at the head of the coffee table, completing a triangle of the three. "Clara, what do you know about how you came to be here?"

She shook her head. "All I know is that I heard a voice tell me that this is my chance for redemption, and then I was in that room with him." She pointed to Ramatel.

"And you were the first to find her?" Gabriel looked at Ramatel.

Ramatel nodded.

"What is the last thing you remember?" Gabriel asked the woman.

Her eyes darted back and forth, then looked up, unfocused, as she shifted through her memories. "I remember... um..." Her look grew distant then her body froze stark still for a moment. They waited quietly for her to recognize any memories while stilled, then she startled violently in the chair, almost leaping off it. "I... I think I was... shot."

Gabriel nodded reassuringly then continued in a soothing tone. "Then what happened?"

She paused, trying to pull memories from her mind. "That's it. That's all I remember."

"No whiteness? No great gates?"

She shook her head.

Gabriel gave a tired sigh. "My dear, I believe you have been in purgatory. We are the angels of earth, and from time to time, the Father chooses to offer those in purgatory a way to heaven by serving angels, so long as he believes they hold some skill or potential that can help our cause."

"You're angels?" the girl repeated in wonder. Her eyebrows shot up.

Ramatel rolled his eyes. *I have better things to do. I should be out hunting.* The girl and Gabriel either ignored him or they didn't catch his eye roll.

"So I died?" she asked.

Gabriel nodded.

"And I didn't make the cut?"

Gabriel shook his head.

The girl's expression became infallible. "I think I knew I was dead…" She trailed off.

"It's likely. Most in purgatory have some idea."

"So this is my chance to make amends?"

"I guess the Father thought you could help in some way. Your kind is called *chinfon* to us, it means something like an addition or extension." Gabriel explained while Ramatel impatiently began to bounce his legs.

"How will I help?"

"Well, we'll have to figure that out. Most stay here and help around the house. Some study for occupations that further the Father's cause while they're here, such as nurses, clergy, teachers, and the like. Then they move on to do that work. Usually the Father directs you to your true calling. Did He say anything else?"

She shook her head. "How long do I have?"

"I suppose as long as it takes. Mostly it's until the Father thinks you have fulfilled your penance or served your purpose."

The woman looked down at her bare arms, apparently taking this all in. "My tattoos are gone," she whispered in disbelief, running her fingers of one hand against her forearm.

"You have been washed clean."

Ramatel almost growled when he heard that. *This human who didn't even make it to heaven is washed clean while I'm left looking like the Phantom of the fucken Opera without the mask!*

Ramatel couldn't even pass his scars off as an unfortunate accident or as war wounds from a knife fight. No, these scars were all specific designs with geometric shapes, arrows, broken crosses, and purposeful lines. Humans who saw him would deduce he was a blade crazed masochist. Angels recognized the symbols and could see evidence of his physical weakness. Ramatel clenched his fist at the thought.

"Washed clean," she repeated as if she was trying the words out for the first time. "Am I an angel too then?"

Gabriel shook his head and offered a condolence smile. "You're something else. Kind of like a lesser angel, but really more like a human. You have no wings, you still get hurt, but you'll heal faster than a human and you won't age while you're here. If you die before your purpose is served you might come back or you might face judgment again. It's up to the Father at that point."

Gabriel anticipated the next question, but then again, he had probably done this orientation thing hundreds of times, Ramatel supposed. Gabriel stood and turned his back to her. Feathery white wings sprouted and magically cut through his shirt without ripping it. It was more like the wings just molded into the clothing. They spread at least six feet in either direction, arched and tapered like bird wings.

Ramatel felt another wave of jealousy. His own wings hadn't fully regained their color. They remain a shade of light grey from all the times in Hell he'd been burned.

The girl stood gaped at the sight, until Gabriel folded his wings down and they disappeared into his back as if they'd never been there.

"You're… Gabriel. Like *the* Gabriel?"

Gabriel nodded and Clara looked like she might pass out. Her face had gone even more pale than it had been before. Ramatel didn't know that was possible.

"I think we had better get you to bed. I'll give you a room until Ramatel can find a place for you."

"What?!" Ramatel fired a look of horror at Gabriel.

"She appeared to you first. That means that she is here to help you, and that she is yours to care for. You're her *chinshen*, and she's your *chinfon*."

"Fuck no! I'm not taking care of a woman!"

"This is the Father's decision."

"I can barely take care of myself!" Ramatel continued to protest.

"Perhaps…" Gabriel said as he led them out of the study, "that's why she is here."

Chapter Two

Clara awoke the next morning with the mental fog of sleep still clouding her mind. It wasn't until she opened her eyes that she realized it hadn't been a dream. She was in a strange house, in the room that a man named Gabriel had put her in. No, not a man. The Archangel Gabriel, with wings and golden eyes and everything. She looked at her forearms and confirmed what she had learned last night. There were still no tattoos.

A knock on the door reminded Clara what had awoken her in the first place, and she jumped to answer it. On the other side of the door she was greeted by an auburn-haired young woman, wearing jeans and a pink t-shirt with a picture of a cat on it.

"Hello!" called the cheerful woman with a bright smile. "I'm Amy. I work here for Gabriel. Isn't he a great guy?!" Her eyes rolled back when she said the word "great" to emphasize her sincerity, but she didn't stop to wait for an answer. "So I heard there was a new girl and I just wanted to invite you to come eat with the staff."

"Um, okay," Clara replied sleepily. "I'll be right down."

Shortly, Clara emerged dressed in clothes that someone had provided that were a tad too large, but sneakers that were just the right size. Amy was still waiting in the hall.

"So welcome back to earth!" She grinned at Clara.

Clara smiled back, and pondered how anyone could be this cheerful this early in the morning. "Thanks."

"I'm surprised he put you in that room. Most of us live on the other side of the house." Amy chirped on.

"I guess it's temporary. I think I'm supposed to go live with that scarred guy... Rama... something."

Amy stopped walking for a brief second, but seemed to catch herself then resumed her pace. "Ramatel?"

"Yeah, that guy."

"Oh." Amy said, in a more serious tone that clued Clara in.

"What?"

"It's just that he's... um..."

"An asshole? Yeah I picked up on that last night."

"That's one description I suppose." Amy led her down a staircase and into the kitchen. There was a small table in a nook with two other women and two men sitting around it. They had coffee mugs and plates of toast and eggs.

"Good Morning!" a dark haired woman greeted her. "I'm Maria. How do you take your eggs?" the woman asked in accented English.

Clara shrugged, not wanting to be a burden to anyone. "Anything is fine."

"Fried is good?" She sounded like she might be from South America.

"Sure."

Clara was ushered to a seat and introduced to the rest of the staff. Brian was the maintenance man, Jeffrey the groundskeeper, and Julie was another cleaning staff like Amy but was taking nursing classes. Maria apparently was the cook, and boy could she cook! Clara had never had a breakfast so amazing and it was just a simple fried egg on toast with bacon.

"This is delicious!" she said as she put the last bite in her mouth. She'd just realized that she eaten everything in under two minutes.

"Thank you!" Maria beamed proudly. "The angels bring the groceries from their travels so everything is always fresh."

Clara listened as the two men talked work for a bit. Brian teased Jeffrey about his uneven lines on the grass. Jeffrey said he was just trying to keep it interesting so no one gets bored.

Maria tsked. "No one has been bored around here for a year." She tilted her head toward the window with the visible back house.

"That's Ramatel's house right?" Clara asked, recognizing the yard she had been led across last night.

"Ramatel, Asael, Barakel, and Sahariel, but at least Sahariel is quiet." Julie answered as she began to clear the dishes from the table.

"Oh. The others aren't?"

"Sahariel hasn't woken up for over a year. No one here has ever seen him awake," Amy answered.

"What's wrong with him?"

Amy shrugged. "Dunno, those guys don't let us spend much time in that house. Not that we want to." Amy turned to the others. "Clara was sent to Ramatel," she announced.

The clinking of dishes stopped and everyone turned to stare at her.

Finally, Jeffrey blew air out of his mouth and raised his eyebrows. "Well good luck with that."

"Why? What should I know?"

Amy answered. "The guys in the back house were the fallen angels. They were rescued from hell a year ago. They don't exactly act like angels but Jahi—that's Michael's wife, you'll meet her—said that they were tortured for about seventy generations."

"Is that where he got the scars?"

"Yup," Brian answered, "and the attitude."

Clara shadowed Amy for most of the day while Amy cleaned. They began downstairs with dusting and vacuuming, then they moved upstairs for the same thing. Amy, it turned out, was quite the chatterbox. Clara didn't mind because it got her mind off the work and filled in a lot of the missing puzzle pieces.

Apparently, there were two archangels living here, Gabriel and Michael, and one risen demon, Jahi, who was Michael's wife. The four angels in the back sounded awful by Amy's description, or at least the three who were up and about. Amy said they were prone to bouts of rage, night terrors, and mostly they tried to keep to themselves. The angels often slept during the day because they went to fight demons around the southwest USA at night. There was some kind of schedule for that.

Amy also said there were three angelings who were also only about a year old, but looked like they were in their twenties or thirties. Jahi had been helping them perfect their flying techniques, Michael had been teaching them to fight, and Gabriel had been teaching them the rest, but Amy didn't know what that was. One of the angelings, Butator, was a computer genius, Hamal could move water, and no one knew what Liwet's special power was. They just agreed that he was creative and had good ideas.

Sometimes the girls hung out with Jahi, who sounded like she was fun. Amy said if she needed anything to ask Jahi. Apparently, the risen demon loved to shop and was always trying to get the women to dress up more, paint their nails, wear designer clothes, etc.

"You'll see what I mean the next time she calls for a girls' night. So what do you think you'll do here?" Amy asked when they were in the midst of folding laundry.

"Um, I don't really know," Clara answered. She meant it, she had no idea what she wanted to do, but it wasn't cleaning for the rest of her life. She didn't look down on those who did. Actually, she was grateful someone was willing to clean, but it wasn't for her.

Memories of her old life were gone, but she remembered the gun that killed her. Clara deduced that she might have been a police officer or something. Maybe military. Maybe part of a drug cartel. Maybe an amazon. Who could say, really?

She had seen weapons in some of the rooms they had vacuumed, and Clara knew what they were. They also brought back the memory of a pistol going off at point blank range. She'd jumped at the memory again, and Amy had to sit her down for a minute until her breathing slowed.

The rest of the weapons felt familiar to her though. She felt drawn to them in some way. *No, cleaning is definitely not for me.* She figured she was some sort of warrior and the gut feeling intensified when Amy led her to the gym.

"Julie asked if we could clean in here. She usually does it but she is studying for a big test."

The gym had wrestling mats, weight lifting equipment, free weights, punching bags, and all manner of martial arts weapons. Clara smiled at the sight of them as if she was coming home to a familiar setting. Amy began to wipe down the machines, trying to manipulate them into alternate positions to clean between the cracks and dust the pulleys. She obviously didn't know how to move them correctly. It couldn't be a coincidence that Clara knew how to operate them all.

"So this is where they train, huh?" Clara asked, trying to prompt for more information about the martial arts weapons.

"Yup, they're all super strong and they keep their bodies in mint condition. It probably helps with the fighting.

"You said they fight demons?"

"Demons and demon cronies." Clara gave her a quizzical look and Amy continued to explain. "A lot of the demons use humans to carry out their work in the world, and we call them cronies. They're like the street gangs and drug cartels, or just generally bad people."

Clara nodded but she was too busy assessing the functionality of the training grounds to reply.

Chapter Three

That evening the staff came together again to eat dinner. Maria had prepared curried lamb with rice and salad. Everyone stopped to wash up. Brian walked in covered with metal shavings and sawdust so Maria sent him to change.

"Oh good. You're here," Gabriel said to Clara as he walked into the kitchen. His tall form made the space seem crowded, but he didn't take notice and neither did anyone else. They were probably used to the giant angel. It was his house after all. "Ramatel said he set up his room for you, and Jahi would like to take you shopping tomorrow." He made a beckoning gesture toward the door and she followed him to the backyard.

"So how are you adjusting?" he asked as they walked across the grass

"Alright. I guess." She all but trotted to keep up with his long strides. *Are all angels this big? That Ramatel guy is.*

"Have you recovered any more memories?" Gabriel slowed the pace for her when he noticed that she was taking two steps to his every one.

"No, but my death has become a little more..." *What's the word?* "Vivid."

"What do you mean?"

Clara looked down, debating whether to tell him that her only memory was terrifying. "I remember a pistol going off in my face."

He nodded, but didn't say anything.

"Does everyone remember their death?"

They were almost to the other house, so he stopped and turned to her so they could finish this conversation before going in. "No, it's unusual. It might be some kind of hint, or it might be nothing. You said you also had tattoos?"

She nodded. "Yeah, sleeves of them. I was thinking maybe I was a cop, or military, or something."

"Yeah, maybe. Hard to tell. We don't even know if you were a man or a woman in your past life."

She stared up in him in shock. He grinned back then turned to step up to the front door and knocked.

Is he serious?

Another giant man answered the door as Clara was bombarded with the sound of screaming that she supposed passed as music to some people. The man stood blocking the doorway with his arms crossed. He had dark hair, cut very close to his head, and dark eyes that matched his hair. His high cheekbones accentuated his brown skin. If she had to guess, he might be Native American or Hispanic. She could feel the intensity of his gaze as he eyed her, probably because Clara was unabashedly staring at him.

His eyebrows were pierced with curved silver dumbbell studs whose top ends were shaped like little horns. His bottom lip was pierced twice and made to look like he had fangs protruding from his lip. Each of his ears had dumbbells connecting the front of the ear to the back of it and numerous other piercings. Despite the heat, he wore long sleeves and black cargo pants that reminded Clara of military fatigues. A tactical, black shoulder holster with a giant knife under each arm guided her eyes downward. His feet were bare and Clara spotted large scars on the tops of each.

"Asael, this is Clara." Gabriel put his arm around her in a comforting way. She didn't realize how tense she was until then. "Clara this is Asael."

The pierced man tipped his chin up for an instant but didn't say anything. He just stepped back allowing them entrance. She followed Gabriel through a common sitting area where there was another similarly dressed massive man sitting on a sofa and nursing a beer. This one had piercing blue eyes, long hair with natural brown highlights, and a full beard and mustache. His beard may once have been trimmed but could use another go at it. He stood and shied away as soon as she spotted him. He started toward a hall across the room, until Gabriel called for him.

"Barakel…" The man froze mid step. "This is Clara."

The fleeing man half turned, gave her a quick nod, then stepped out of sight. Gabriel led her in the opposite direction, back toward the room she had appeared in last night. Someone turned the "music" down and she caught the gist of a conversation behind her between the two men. They were placing bets about whether she or Ramatel would leave first.

Clara walked into the room that would have been vaguely familiar to her if not for the fact that it now resembled a child's attempt at a fort. There were flowered sheets hanging from ropes that had not been there the night before. The ropes sectioned off the room, splitting it into two spaces.

On one side of the room a new twin sized bed, dresser, and floor lamp had been added. The other side of the room was occupied by the large king sized bed that had been there the day before, and the common ground held a desk and chair.

Ramatel stood with his arms crossed in his own black fatigues with two large knives strapped to a black utility style belt under his arms, scowling at her. "Happy?" he fired at her as if making an accusation.

Gabriel cleared his throat and answered for her. "It's not exactly what I had in mind—"

Ramatel interrupted him. "If she wants the fucken Hilton she's got the wrong angel."

Clara felt the sudden need to defend her humility and decided to pipe in. "Works for me."

Gabriel gave her an uncertain glance to question her decision. Then, as if to reassure her, he added "It's just until Brian can build you something permanent. He is working on something at the moment. It shouldn't be long."

"I'll be fine."

"She could always go back to your place," Ramatel suggested.

So that's what this is about. He's thinking if he did a crappy job of this I'll just head back over there. She did want to be back over at the other house with friendly faces and classical music, but she also didn't want to give in to his manipulation. She didn't know why, but she sensed that she should stand her ground with this guy.

"I'm okay here."

Gabriel turned to her and put his hands on her shoulders. "If you need anything, or if they scare you at all…" She saw Ramatel roll his eyes and turn away. "…you just come and find me. Okay?"

"I will."

He smiled at her. "Good." He eyed the small bed that was to the left of the doorway. There was a laundry bag sitting on some sheets and blankets. "It looks like the staff packed some things for you. Tomorrow Jahi will meet you after breakfast and take you shopping for clothes and anything else you need."

"Thank you."

He gave her one last look, and she read admiration and pride in it. It was the kind of look you give someone who is about to risk their life to do something very important.

What the hell have I gotten myself into? He pulled her into a hug. *Yup, I'm a dead woman.* Then he bid them goodnight and left.

As soon as they were alone together, Ramatel eyed her up and down, then he grabbed a black leather jacket from a desk chair, and headed for the door but stopped just short. "If you come back early tomorrow, the laundry basket is right over there. Washing machine is in Gabriel's house."

Chapter Four

The angry guy stayed out until about four in the morning. Clara only knew he returned because the clunk of his boots as he took them off woke her. She didn't want to draw any attention to herself, even though he was behind his hung sheet, so she held still. He must have had some kind of a light source that let her see his shadow on the sheet. It was bright and aimed, probably the flashlight feature of a cell phone she decided. The guilt she felt at watching him undress was overshadowed by her need for more information about her new roommate.

He pulled off his shirt and she caught the outline of an extremely powerful body. The silhouette hid the scars she knew were there, but even the scars couldn't hide the fact that he was a magnificent specimen. His muscles were like hard rocks below his skin. Even through the sheet she could see his muscles ripple as he moved. There wasn't an extra pound of fat on him anywhere.

She thought back to the moment she had first seen him. Even with the scars his face was handsome. He had likely been stunningly beautiful before he was damaged, and she wondered what had happened in hell. Surely nothing good. Her mind didn't wander there long because he began unbuckling his belt. His pants dropped to the floor with a thud from something heavy in his pockets and she was treated to a shadow show of taut masculinity.

His wide shoulders and bulging biceps radiated power. Those narrow hips of his hovered above brawny powerful thighs. She felt the beginning of a smile creep along her lips, then she remembered the comment he made

about laundry before he left. *Too bad he's such an asshole.*
She closed her eyes and drifted back to sleep.

　　She awoke around seven, showered, dressed, and
headed to the main house for breakfast. It looked like the
back house she lived in only had a tiny little kitchenette
with no food to speak of; although, it was well-stocked
with vodka, whiskey, and tequila. The rest of the staff
were already finishing their breakfasts when she joined
them. Maria put a plate in front of her while others loitered
enjoying their coffee. They warned her not to expect Jahi
until at least nine o'clock. No one said they needed help,
and from the conversation it sounded like the angels had
all had a late night and were sleeping it off, so Clara stole
away to the gym.

　　The familiar smell of the wrestling mats, equipment
oil, and sweat, all mingled together, hit her as she opened
the door. The aroma made her smile, but she couldn't
remember why. She picked a pair of rattan sticks that were
about two feet long and an inch wide out of a box with
other practice weapons. With one in each hand she felt
powerful. She pushed them alternately through an
imaginary opponent's head in front of her, listening to the
swooshing sounds they made as they cut through the air.
She twisted her hips in tune with the sticks, pivoting on the
balls of her feet.

　　She knew how to chamber one stick while the other
was in use. She knew to hold them a good five to six
inches from the base so she could use both sides of the
stick if need be. She knew if someone grabbed the stick
she could trap their hand and push the bottom of her stick
over their wrist to create a painful hold, but she had no
idea how she knew these things.

She threw a practice block and followed it with a kick at this imaginary foe, who was fortunately very slow in his attack.

I was definitely a ninja in my past life. Was Gabriel kidding when he said I might have been a man? She looked at her blank forearms again as if they were the key to unlocking a mystery, but, try as she might, she couldn't envision what image her tattoos had consisted of.

She found a martial arts dummy that had seen better days. It was a torso of a man on a punching bag stand. The whole thing appeared to be held together with duct tape, and it looked like the dummy had been beheaded on numerous occasions then stuck back together. She assumed a stance with her feet apart, placed one stick in front of her defensively and hid the other behind her back so her dummy opponent wouldn't be able to gage the length of the stick behind her. Then she launched herself at the dummy, sticks flying and dealing what would be, at best, many bruises or a concussion. At worst, broken limbs and serious head trauma.

"That's wonderful! Michael is going to love you!" came a feminine voice behind her.

Clara turned to see a stunningly gorgeous woman with long, loose, straight black hair behind her. The woman was at least a head taller than she, and wore stiletto heels that added even more height. She was wearing a red dress that looked like it had come off a Barbie doll, and wore a matching shade of lipstick. Next to this supermodel, Clara felt like a kid dressed in her big brother's clothes.

"Hi! I'm Jahi," the model held out her hand.

"Clara." She shook the outstretched hand.

"It's nice to meet you. Where did you learn to do that?" Jahi asked, pointing to the dummy.

"Um, I don't know. I don't remember much from my old life."

"Oh, that sucks. Well, Michael will love it. He thinks everyone should know how to fight, although it's not going to help my cause of avoiding it. Fighting just isn't really my thing." Jahi grinned and Clara smiled back.

Blaring upbeat dance music for all to hear, they left the estate in a candy-apple-red, convertible Ferrari, with a license plate that read "Hell Rsn." Despite Jahi's attempts to steer them to Rodeo Drive, they ended up at the mall with a Target, where Clara had done most of her shopping.

"You look like a boy," Jahi whined when Clara emerged from a dressing room in beige hiking pants and a plain shirt.

"I don't think it matters what I wear, I'm just here to save my soul. No one is going to be looking at me."

"Not if you dress like that they won't be. Here," Jahi handed Clara a dress that was little more than a wash cloth. "Try this on."

Clara eyed it suspiciously. "It… um… doesn't leave much to the imagination."

"That's the point!" Jahi beamed. "If you got it, flaunt it!"

"I don't 'got it' though."

"Sure you do. You just don't know it because it's all covered up right now."

Clara sighed and grabbed the dress. She had to admit she looked good. Even though she had no idea what kind of servitude she was supposed to be doing, she figured that any servitude that involved dressing like this probably wasn't the Lord's cause.

"You look great! Spin around!" Jahi grinned when Clara stepped out of the dressing room.

"I don't think I should waste Gabriel's money on something I probably won't wear."

"Are you kidding? You'll wear it when we go out dancing. Don't worry about the money, the Father provides. They just wave their hands and create it out of thin air. Guess it's an angel thing." Jahi drifted off into thought, peering at the door of the store's mall entrance. Then she shot Clara an evil grin. "Let's go lingerie shopping!"

Clara and Jahi stayed out all day, though not all of it was shopping. They'd picked up lunch at a nice little Italian deli and picnicked in a park where Jahi seemed oblivious to the stares from men she received. Clara used the break to dig for information about Ramatel.

According to Jahi, he and the others had only been rescued from hell about a year ago. Jahi seemed reluctant to talk about what hell was like, but she said they were there because the Father had punished them for sleeping with human women.

"They have more in common with demons than they do angels. Trust me, I should know. They're getting better though, well except Sahariel who hasn't woken up yet. It took them a good week to speak and a month to sleep in beds. They're aren't evil though, probably. I've never seen them actually hurt anyone besides the demons. They do like to scare the crap out of people sometimes, but I think that's just their coping mechanisms or something."

Clara raised her eyebrows.

"Don't worry, God wouldn't have sent you here if you couldn't handle him."

Great...

They got home a little after seven that night and Maria had saved them each a plate for dinner. There was a huge gorgeous man with long blonde hair and the same golden eyes as Gabriel waiting for them when they walked in. Jahi greeted him with an emphatic kiss that was so passionate it made Clara blush. She turned away trying to get her mind off the voyeuristic prone scene in front of her and wondered why the fallen angels didn't have golden eyes.

"Hi! I'm Michael," a deep voice called from behind her. She spun around.

"Show him what you can do!" Jahi cried excitedly before Clara could answer. Jahi turned to Michael. "She can fight!"

"Can she?" he asked in an indiscernible tone. "Show me."

Any confidence she thought she had suddenly left her at the expectation of demonstrating her ninja moves. She'd only played around because she thought she was alone.

"Come on!" Jahi was leading them to the gym already.

When they opened the door to the gym she saw two men she hadn't met before on the wrestling mat grappling with each other. One was black with dark hair and golden eyes, and one was fair skinned with bright red hair. Both, of course, were well built with corded muscles that radiated strength. These two weren't as big as Michael,

Gabriel, or Ramatel though. They didn't pause the match as Clara and Jahi proceeded by them. Their bodies entwined until one of them held the other pinned, then an escape was launched.

"Hamal and Butator," Jahi explained as they walked by. "Liwet is on duty with Asael and Barakel." Jahi guided them over to the dummy Clara had been beating earlier that day when Clara glimpsed Ramatel at a weight lifting bench pushing an enormous amount of weight in the corner.

A whole audience… ugh.

"Here," Jahi handed her the sticks she had used.

Clara heard a clink as Ramatel set down the bar of weights he'd been lifting. She could feel that all eyes were on her now and her nerves were revving up. "Um, I'd rather not." The grappling match had ended and the two men stared on. Ramatel was sitting up, giving her his usual glare.

"It's okay," Michael encouraged. "Let's just see where you are at."

She glanced at Ramatel again. He stood up and crossed his bulging arms. When she looked at his face, he pinched his lips together in a thin line and shook his head, then turned back to the bench to resume his workout. At seeing his reaction, her apprehension was replaced by anger, and she reached for the sticks with resolve. She was going to do this just to spite him.

"Alright, stand back."

She launched herself at the dummy as she had that morning, but this time she had the fury of disproving the chauvinistic angel by the weight bench to spur her on. She twisted and turned, attacking the various weak points of the body from both directions. She beat the dummy for all her worth until one of her sticks suddenly met with another stick before she could make contact with the next strike point.

Michael had picked up his own and was inviting her to spar. She turned without breaking her rhythm and began both attacking him and fighting off his attacks.

As their sticks met over and over she felt the wave of every impact through her hands and wrists, but she fought on. She could sense that he was holding a lot back. That didn't matter to her though. It was still the most fun she'd had on earth yet. She felt herself smiling as they danced across the mats. She'd push forward then be driven back. She'd deflect blows and drive her own, then defend herself until she found another opening.

Finally, after what must have been ten minutes, she was winded and began to slow. Michael stepped back and bowed, indicating the fight was over. She returned the bow and beamed when Jahi and the two angels she didn't know clapped from the sidelines. Even Gabriel had joined them in the gym at some point.

"Where did you learn to do that?" Michael asked.

"I don't know. I don't remember," she shrugged but glanced at Gabriel. "I was going to ask if maybe instead of cleaning I could help fight?"

"Well I'm on board," Michael said enthusiastically. "But that's a discussion between you and your *chinshen.*"

Fuck.

She shot the scarred man a hopeful glance.

"Absolutely not. She's too weak, she'd get killed in a day."

Asshole. "I can get stronger."

"You're as good as a human. You'll never be strong enough to take on a demon."

Gabriel spoke up before this could turn into a full blown yelling match. "Ramatel may I have a word with you outside?"

Ramatel followed Gabriel out of the gym door. Michael gave her a reassuring smile then pulled the other two men to the side and began correcting a move and demonstrating some hold.

Jahi stepped close to Clara. She closed her eyes and appeared to be concentrating really hard. "Gabriel is saying that if it's your calling then Ramatel doesn't have a choice. Ramatel thinks it's preposterous for a woman to fight and says he can't protect you."

"You can hear them?"

Jahi nodded then put her lips to her fingers with a smile. "Ramatel says you're too weak and small and too close to being human."

Jahi paused a moment, waiting for the conversation outside to move forward. "Gabriel says it doesn't matter and that Lord has revealed your talent, and that Ramatel can't stop you because you have free will. Ramatel says he won't be responsible if you get killed. Then Gabriel asked if that means Ramatel is going to train you so you don't get killed." She cocked her head. "Ramatel said he is going to forbid you from fighting and Gabriel said he can't take away your free will or you will not face judgement." Jahi paused. "Ramatel is leaving. I think Gabriel won that argument."

Hours later, after a few more rounds with Michael, Clara returned to the room she shared with Ramatel only to find a radio blasting that angry screaming music again.

Someone had pulled her sheet/wall aside and put her shopping bags on her bed with a highly visible giant red Frederick's of Hollywood bag right on top of the pile. She felt her cheeks blush with the idea that anyone would think she had bought sexy underwear. It wasn't even her bag. It was Jahi's. She grabbed the bag and began to walk out of the room intending to deliver it to its rightful owner.

"Jahi dropped that off, said it was a welcome gift," growled the scarred man who was lounging on the king sized bed with a drink in his hand. Clara jumped at the sound of his voice. She hadn't noticed him at first because it was so dark in that corner.

Clara looked at the bag. She couldn't imagine what kind of things someone like Jahi would feel were appropriate welcome presents. "Thank you," she said, and stepped inside her curtained area, pulling the sheet shut.

"It's never going to work, you know," he called across the room.

She re-emerged from her sheeted off room. "What?"

"Fighting, it's not going to work."

Clara took a breath and readied herself for all the anti-women-in-combat arguments to come her way. "Why's that?"

Ramatel put his drink down and strolled over to her. "Give me your hand." He held out his own, palm up, almost in a romantic gesture. Damn he smelled good. She had no idea how long she was in purgatory, but she must not have been getting any for a long time.

She tentatively put hers in his and looked up to meet his eyes. She wasn't sure what she was hoping to find there. Maybe interest. Maybe kindness or a smile. Appreciation even. But whatever she was looking for, she didn't find it. His dark eyes glared at her. She started to pull her hand back and he tightened the grip making her attempts feeble.

He pulled a tiny pocketknife from some hidden place with his free hand and the blade sprung open. Clara began struggling in earnest now.

"Wait, just hold still. You need to see this." He put the blade to his own forearm and made a small cut on the skin, just enough for a drop of golden blood to come out. Then the blade headed for her arm. She tried to pull away again.

"Stop!" he commanded. "Watch." He ran the blade along her forearm making a cut the same size.

"Ow!"

Ramatel shot her a "spare me the dramatics" look and released her hand. "Look," he said and held up his own arm. The cut was gone as if it had never existed. "Now watch how long it takes your cut to heal. You heal faster than a human, but you're no match for a demon who heals like I do. I can take a bullet to the heart and heal in minutes, you'd just die."

He stepped away from her and she eyed her own cut. The blood was dried already, but it still hurt.

"Don't worry," he said, turning to resume his lurking on his side of the room. "You won't even have a scar there in about twenty minutes," he snarled bitterly.

"Maybe I can just fight the humans then. What do you call them? Cronies? Maybe I can just help with support or something. There's gotta to be a place for me somewhere."

He shrugged his shoulders but didn't turn around, mumbling something about a woman's place. Clara got the

impression that, according to him, this subject was dead,
so she returned to her room, such as it was, and closed the
sheet. She began to fold her new clothes and put them
away until finally, the only bag left to empty was the one
Jahi had left. The pain in her arm was gone and Ramatel
had been right, the thing had healed already.

Chapter Five

Ramatel had been stewing in the corner. His anger was wavering as he watched the shadow of her form on the thin sheet as she pulled things out of the bag Jahi had left. Whatever they were, there wasn't much material, and he couldn't help but imagine how she would look wearing so little material. Once she held something up to herself as if picturing it on her then laughed and shook her head.

She turned off her floor lamp and began to strip, but the lights from outside the window still provided a nice view of her outline. She probably had no idea that angels has such great night vision. His botched up attempt to keep her at Gabriel's was proving to be serendipitous.

He watched her remove her shirt and held his breath as she pulled her bra from her body. Her full breasts were high with youth and peaked with tiny little nipples that must have been pebbled and tight given how they stood out from her body.

Ramatel felt himself hardening under his pants and rearranged himself. He hated that she had that much control over him without even knowing it, but he still couldn't look away. Every instinct in him roared against relinquishing any control over his body. A lack of control led to pain, and he had learned that lesson well in hell.

His thoughts were brought back to the present when she eased her jeans over her bottom and pulled them down. He had to suppress a groan. Her curvy but petite figure was all but displayed, and he couldn't do anything about it. There had once been a time when he had been so beautiful that he could have any maiden he wanted, back when maidens had willingly taken care of the home and let the men do the fighting and hunting.

What was he supposed to do with a woman who wouldn't want his scarred, sorry ass in bed but wanted to do the fighting herself? He supposed he should try treating her like a man, but one look at those breasts undid any hope of that. Ramatel was in uncharted water; it was riddled with sharks. His last relationship landed him in hell for more than two thousand years.

"Can you turn the music down? I'm going to go to bed," she called.

Here one day and already demanding I change my habits. He assumed a mocking tone. "If you think you're going to be a fighter you better get used to our schedule. Demons come out at night."

She gave an exasperated sigh. "Fine." She opened her bed sheet dressed now in satin pajamas.

He pulled his knees up to hide his arousal. He had to get her away from him. "That should give you plenty of time to do the laundry."

She narrowed her eyes at him and set her jaw forward with obvious displeasure. Her arms crossed in front of her chest and she seemed to be considering something. "Ask me nicely."

"What?" *Did this least of the angelic ranks just back talk me? Even the lesser angels of earth have more respect than that. That insolent little—*

"Ask me nicely."

"You're supposed to be here to help, I shouldn't have to ask."

"I am helping. I'm teaching you some manners."

He rose from the bed, anger having taken care of his arousal better than anything he could have done himself, and stalked closer to her. To her credit, she didn't back up. He moved until he was inches from her tiny little frame. "And I'm about to teach you some respect. You are the least of the angel ranks, and you will respect your elders, little girl."

He reached for her wrists and pushed them both into his left hand, then flashed her back to his side of the room with him sitting on the edge of the bed. With her disorientation and his superior strength, Ramatel was easily able to pull her across his lap. He brought his hand up high and shot it down across her backside. She yelped. The satin did nothing to protect her skin. He knew he had to curb his own power to keep from hurting her.

He raised his hand again and this time struck her other cheek while she squeaked and tried to wriggle free. He alternated cheeks with four more swats and would have kept going if he hadn't smelled something in the air that he was not expecting. Something sweet that he hadn't smelled for a very long time.

Arousal.

He stopped mid-swing. She was getting aroused by this and his body was responding. Or maybe vice versa. He felt the warmth of her body on his crotch and the pressure of her touch was exciting him. He looked down at her round little bottom on display for his perusal if he wanted. The satin hugged her skin, stretched over the round little bottom on his lap.

Losing control.

Ramatel pushed her from his lap as fast as he could, hoping she hadn't noticed his reaction. She sat up from the

floor slightly stunned and glared up at him. He pointed to
the laundry basket. "Now," he commanded.

"Ask me nicely."

He raised his hand again in a spanking gesture,
threatening to hit her again.

Instead of flinching and cowering she stuck out her
chin as if to challenge him. "I can do this all night."

He couldn't though, not without her noticing the
bulge in his pants. Grabbing his drink, he fled the room,
draining his glass and ditching it on a coffee table as he
stalked out to the front lawn clenching his fists. He began
to pace back and forth on the grass.

*Confounding woman! She thinks she can play games
with me!* He stopped to readjust his swollen cock and
pondered the effect she'd had on him. In the year that he'd
been back he hadn't felt anything even close to desire for
anyone. One day with her here, and he already needed to
rub one out. Frustrated, he headed back to the gym to
finish the workout she had interrupted, then maybe he'd
start another one.

Several hours later, after a workout that Ramatel had
hoped would take the edge off his vexation, he made his
way to the back house. It was still empty when he opened
the door, although this should have been about the time his
brothers would come back from their hunting. *Must have
been a busy night.* He walked the hallway leading back to
his room but stopped himself with his hand on the
doorknob.

Ramatel cloaked himself before he entered so he'd
be invisible to her eyes. He told himself it was so he
wouldn't wake her, but after the shadow play he'd seen
earlier, even he doubted his own intentions. The

temptation was too much for him. He turned the doorknob and slipped inside.

Her sheet was drawn and he could hear the slow rhythm of her breathing. With an outstretched hand he silently drew the sheet aside, opening up her room.

She wore the same satin pajamas he'd seen earlier and was covered with blankets up to her waist. She lay on her stomach with her face was toward him. Even in the dim light from the window he could see the freckles that covered every inch of her face. A strand of hair fell across her forehead and he brushed it aside. A partial smiled crossed her face in her sleep when he touched her, but he knew that smile wasn't for him. Someone like her didn't belong with a scarred piece of meat like him, roasted by the fires of hell. He'd proven that tonight.

But then again, she'd been aroused hadn't she? Maybe he was mistaking the scent. It had been so long since he'd smelled it. Thousands of years ago he'd have known that smell in an instant... and he wouldn't have hesitated.

The hand he'd touched her face with recoiled to his own. He felt the raised flesh of the scars there. Each scar was the moniker of the demons who tortured him, whomever was the victor in the game of who could break him the fastest. With every new record set he'd received a new scar. His endurance and strength had led them to challenge each other. Now when he looked in the mirror their personal designs served as reminder of his weakness during his stint in the abyss, their command over his body. He didn't know how many scars he wore, he never bothered to count, but it had to be hundreds.

She murmured something unintelligible that may or may not have been a word, and rolled to her back. He caught that scent again briefly as the blankets shifted. Her breasts pressed against the satin pajama shirt. He longed to caress them and feel the softness of her skin. He wished he could treat her tenderly, but he couldn't. All he could be now was hard. He had lost any tenderness he once had in the pit.

His fingers still crossed over the lines on his face. Within an arm's length was a beautiful woman, one he would like to have, but it was never going to happen. He was ugly now. Ugly from his punishment from God. His hand clenched into a fist.

Seventy fucken generations of pain, torment, and torture for disobeying one order. *One!* Michael fucked a goddammed demon and didn't even get some much as a tsk tsk, but Ramatel slept with human women and got over two thousand years of torture with the scars to last eternity!

Rage hit him like a full speed train and he jumped back, taking the sheet with him. He caught himself and spun away from her, trying protect her from the danger he could feel coursing through his veins as his anger boiled over. The unfairness, the wrong of it, filled his body with an energy that needed an outlet immediately. Before he had a chance to think, his mouth opened in a roar and his hands had smashed through the desk chair. He picked up a chair leg and beat what was left of the chair until it was a pile of splintered wood.

He heard a stifled cry behind him and turned to see her backed into a corner on her bed, clutching the blankets to her chest. Her eyes were wide with fear. Her mouth was partially opened and her eyebrows were high. He knew that his invisibility cloak had dissolved, probably when the rage overtook him.

Shit, now I scared her. I can't even be a decent chinshen. *Everything I come into contact with I ruin.*

Hard.

That was all he was now. Hard and scarred. He tried to mumble something like "Sorry," but he wasn't sure if it actually came out or not, then he left the room.

Chapter Six

Clara had gone to bed with a feeling of accomplishment and a sore backside. As she lay there she relived the thrill of the spanking. She didn't know why it aroused her, maybe it was the strip tease she'd gotten the night before, maybe it was just being on a man's lap, maybe it was his own excitement that she'd responded to. Whatever it was, she imagined many different endings to that scenario than what had actually happened.

What would it have been like if he'd let his hand explore after the last swat to her behind? She pictured him soothing the pain away, and more.

But then what the hell happened in the middle of the night? Was he really that pissed off over laundry? If so, that made her even more determined not to give in. She was not going reward a temper tantrum. He hadn't come back that night, so eventually she just returned to sleep.

Michael had invited her to join in their training, so for the next week she reported to him alone. He said he would catch her up to the "kids," who appeared to be older than her, and then she would jump in with them when she was at their level.

Her mornings usually began with weight lifting, running, or swimming followed by empty handed grappling. It was clear she'd had training at some point, but those sticks were apparently her strong suit, grappling was not. She would train throughout the day and help out the house staff if she had a break. The laundry basket in her room however remained in place, as steadfast as her resolve.

Ramatel hadn't said a word to her since the night he spanked her, actually he'd barely even set foot in their room. He had begun sleeping on the sofa in the living room, although it sounded like sometimes he had nightmares. She studied him during his nightly workouts when she was training with Michael, and when she saw him at dinner, where she now ate with the angels. Gabriel said he'd prefer for everyone to eat together but his *chinfons* declined, with various reasons about the schedule of the work they'd chosen, or something. Clara wondered if it was to avoid the fallen, but she could make no such excuses if she was training to fight like them.

Still, Ramatel ensured they were never alone together. If she tried to make conversation he either deflected the attention to someone else, offered vague answers, or pretended he hadn't heard her. She wasn't really sure what to make of him, but his obvious disdain for her was really starting to piss her off.

It's not like she had chosen him to be her *chin-whatever.* If he was mad because she'd chosen to be a fighter and not a subservient docile woman, then he was basically mad at her for being herself. *And fuck him.* She was not going to change. She had little idea of who she was, but at least she knew fighting was for her and cleaning wasn't. If he had a problem with that, he could pout for the rest of his life for all she cared.

This Thursday and Friday were his nights off this week, which probably meant that he would be home those days, and Clara wasn't looking forward to the quality time. Fortunately, Jahi had invited her to go clubbing on Thursday night. None of the other girls ever wanted to go with her because Amy didn't like staying up late, Julie didn't like crowds, and Maria said she was too old for that.

Jahi made a face when she relayed that. "Can you believe that? I'm like a hundred times older than she is. She just doesn't appreciate how great these modern times are. Last time I was on earth it was all modesty and mud."

Clara had opted to get ready for their outing in Jahi's room because she suspected Ramatel was in theirs at the moment. Plus she didn't own any makeup. Jahi picked a chiffon mini dress with a neckline that plunged almost down to her belly button, barely covering breasts that Clara could tell were what plastic surgeons tried to emulate with their procedures.

Clara was a little less confident in the staying ability of something so revealing—and in her own tomboy-ish figure—so she chose a pair of black leather pants, heeled combat boots, and was reaching for her shirt when Jahi stopped her.

"Oh no you don't! If you're going out with me, you gotta dress to have a good time and not like you're going into battle. Here, put this on."

Jahi handed Clara a bright red "shirt" that, instead of solid material, had only strings crisscrossing down the back. The front consisted of two triangles to cover her breasts and a two inch strip of material below that. It was really more of a glorified bikini top.

"Um…" Clara began to protest.

"Just try it on," Jahi insisted.

Several hours later they departed with their hair curled, their make-up heavy, and their clothes scant. Jahi had won the battle over the "shirt," but allowed Clara a transparent cover up and a jacket "as long as the jacket is just for the car ride." They had to drive again because of Clara's inability to teleport. Jahi couldn't take her, she said it was only the strongest angels who possessed the ability to transport others.

"It takes a lot of energy to do that, and the further you go, the more energy it takes. Archangels are strong and old so they can move others, but I'm not *that* old."

They arrived at the Lure Nightclub around ten that night. Clara followed Jahi to the door, past all the humans waiting in line to get in. A dark brunette man with a smoking hot body and a tempting face eyed them as they bypassed the line. He had thick eyebrows, a strong jaw, a roman nose, and a tempting look. Clara shot him an embarrassed smile as she trailed Jahi who just hugged the bouncer like they were old friends and walked right inside, with Clara on her heels determined not to lose her.

Inside, the club was packed with dancing bodies and thumping music. Balls of glowing light hung from the ceiling and neon filled the room. There was a live DJ spinning music at one end of the place and a bar on the other. Jahi danced her way through the pool of bodies bumping each other on the dance floor and brought them to a patio with a reserved cabana booth, decorated in a brilliant green, and raised a step above the ground, where they already had bottle service awaiting them.

Jahi poured them each a vodka and cranberry, with a little less cranberry and more vodka than Clara would have preferred, but Clara didn't say anything, she just decided she'd sip it slowly.

"Cheers!" Jahi held up her glass. "To your revival!"

They clinked glasses together and sipped. "So…" Jahi asked when they set their drinks down, "what's with you and Ramatel?"

Clara gave her a confused look. "What do you mean?"

"The tension between you two is so thick you couldn't cut it with a hacksaw. It's hard not to notice. He stares at you when you're not looking, you drool when he's working out. What's going on?"

"I do not drool!" Clara protested.

"Ugh huh… You forget that erotic expressions were my profession. You can't fool me, you're hot for him!"

"I am not! He's an asshole! Did you know he threw a tantrum when I wouldn't do his laundry and spanked me like a child?"

Jahi grinned at her. "Are you sure it wasn't like a role playing game?"

"I'm sure," Clara grumbled and took another drink. "You know the fucked up part?" she asked, looking away from Jahi in shame. "I would have done it if he'd just said please. He just refuses to be anything but a dickhead to me." She took another sip of her drink. "Actually, I'm pretty sure he hates me."

"No way he hates you. I've seen how he looks at you, and that's not hate. That's want."

"Oh he hates me, he even cut me with a knife."
"What?!"

"Yeah, he wanted to show me how weak and pathetic I am, and how slow I heal compared to him, so he cut my arm with a knife."

"Well, tact might not be one of his virtues, but he still wants you. I know that look on a man's face."

Clara took another sip and raised an eyebrow. "I think you're misreading it."

Jahi gave her a skeptical eye narrow but didn't pursue it. "Okay, well then this place if filled with juicy sweet candy, maybe we can find you a lollipop to lick. Let's go dance!" As Jahi refilled their glasses and Clara realized that she hadn't sipped slowly at all, then she allowed Jahi to drag her to the dance floor.

Chapter Seven

Across town, Liwet and Asael were following Barakel's direction to someplace in Long Beach. Liwet had received a text with an address on it and, thanks to mapping apps, was able to head that way. Asael was right behind him as they flew. Modern technology was still a foreign concept to Asael, but mostly because he stubbornly refused to try, so the navigation was up to Liwet.

At least he was allowed to contribute something.

Liwet's phone alerted him. "Area's hot," the text from Barakel read, meaning danger up ahead. The phone chirped again with the new location of a meeting spot, which turned out to be the north end of a ship yard.

Barakel was waiting alone in a parking lot with his typical stern countenance that remained unchanged as they landed. His beard hid any slight expressions he may have made. In fact, the only sign of any potential threat was the fact that he had a large hunting dagger in each hand. Despite this, he waited underneath a bright street light in the open.

Liwet and Asael tucked their wings when they landed and approached the stoic man.

"Whatchu got?" Asael asked.

"A whole horde, maybe ten or twelve. Living out of the ISO containers in the shipyard."

"Should we call for backup?" Liwet asked, pushing up the bandana that was holding back his long brown hair, and furrowing his eyebrows over his golden eyes.

The others gave him a sharp look indicating that was a preposterous idea.

"It's only twelve," Barakel reminded him.

Asael slapped him on the back with a grin. "Don't worry little buddy you gotta get your dagger wet sometime."

Liwet wanted to remind them that his dagger saw plenty of action the night he'd helped rescue them from the pit, but he bit his tongue. They were thousands of years older than he was after all. "Fine," he muttered. "What's the plan?"

"I'll lead you in from the west, they won't be expecting anything to come from the ocean, but we gotta stay cloaked 'cause the containers open in that direction. There's two containers, one on top of the other. They're in the two highest in the stack. I'll take the top container, Asael take the bottom, and Liwet, you kill anything that tries to escape either one."

Liwet was a little insulted that he was essentially just the cleanup crew, but, again, he held back his thoughts. Liwet and Asael drew their own blades and together the three re-sprouted wings and leapt into the air. Liwet followed them over the ocean and cloaked himself in invisibility when they did, which was as soon as they turned and headed for mainland. Barakel was gesturing toward some group of containers when Liwet caught the whiff of demon and felt his adrenaline sky rocket in anticipation of the fight to come.

They picked up speed as they flew and Barakel and Asael each shot into their respective containers like bullets while Liwet slowed and landed on a container to the side. The containers rocked and swayed, filled with noises of the assault as demons were butchered inside. Cries of surprise turned to screams of agony and fear as things bumped and thudded. One did manage to escape the bottom container, and Liwet launched himself at the demon. The thing didn't even turn around as he drove his blade into its back.

Just as Liwet managed to wrench his dagger free of the demon's ribcage another zipped past him from the top container. Liwet beat his wings to gain on the fleeing demon, but only managed to grab its ankle. The demon kicked and pulled but eventually Liwet managed to drag it to the top of the next pile of containers, about ten feet away. He landed first and got his footing while still clinging hard to the ankle of the demon that was thumping its wings in the air. Liwet stabbed it in the thigh just for the sake of injuring it and hoping to slow its fight.

The demon cried out and lashed at him with its fists, catching Liwet on the cheek and eye. Liwet ignored the barrage of punches and pulled the blade down, hauling the demon down with it even further before jerking the blade from its leg. When the demon finally landed on the container, Liwet forced his blade through its chest with a cry of energy and frustration, and the demon's angry expression shifted to shock just before it went limp.

Liwet let the body fall off his blade to the top of container where the body would disintegrate within the hour. Then he returned to the spot he'd left in his pursuit of the demon and was taken aback at a new sound filling the air. The fighting had ceased and a wail rang from the container.

"Liwet! Liwet get in here!" Barakel called, with more urgency than Liwet had ever heard from him.

He cautiously and quickly approached, unsure of what he would find. The stench of demons was overwhelming when he came upon the scene of destruction. Five bodies were sprawled on the floor of the container in various positions, all with black blood oozing from them, but in the back of the container was a pink playpen where the noise was coming from. Liwet and Barakel both sidled up slowly. Liwet had never heard of demon babies before, but who knew what is possible. He peered over the edge of playpen. A bundle of blankets swaddled a very upset, very human, little baby.

"Okay, now you can call Gabriel," Asael said behind him.

***

Clara danced with Jahi, swaying and bouncing to the music, her movements lubricated considerably by the drink in her hand. It felt good to dance and let go of her reservations. Clara could feel the alcohol loosening her thoughts and felt herself grinning without cause. She let the music guide her body while Jahi twirled seductively around the dance floor.

They soon caught the attention of many ogling eyes, and the alcohol ensured that Clara didn't mind. She smiled back and even waved at the sexy man they'd passed in line. He winked in return but did not approach the two. Eventually, they were both sweaty and needed a break, along with a refill of their drinks, despite the fact that, by Clara's count, she had already had three. She started to lead them back to their table, but Jahi put a hand on her shoulder.

"I'll meet you back there, I need to hit the bathroom," Jahi called over the bass that was ringing their ears. Clara nodded as Jahi disappeared into the crowd, then made her way back to the patio. The brunette man was now leaning against the railing on a ramp that led out. He fell into step just behind her as Clara walked by, trying to pretend not to notice him.

"I'd offer to buy you a drink, but it looks like you two have that taken care of," he said, announcing his presence with a confident grin when Clara sat down. "Although you might want this too." He offered a bottle of water.

Clara hadn't realized how thirsty she was for water until she saw the bottle, then she immediately regarded him with a grateful smile. "Thank you." She took it and drained half of it, spilling a few drops down her chest. She felt the man's eyes follow the drops, but couldn't make her spinning mind care.

"I'm Clara," she said, extending her hand for a shake.

"Tanus," he replied, meeting her eyes with a seductive gaze that made Clara swoon. He reached for her hand, but instead of shaking it, he gently lifted it to his lips, only to brush them across the top. He didn't release her hand either, he held it, running his thumb over the back of it while he watched her expression.

"Your skin is so smooth Clara. Is the rest of you as soft as this?"

She felt herself blush and pulled her hand back, but she couldn't think of a comeback or even a reply. She really was having difficulty thinking at all, at least about anything other than this man's touch.

The man stepped closer to where she stood at the edge of the booth, blocking her escape, but she wasn't exactly looking for one. "Your lips look like they may match your hands in softness. Let me test my theory." He lifted her chin up to him with a slight nudge of his hooked forefinger, and pressed his lips to hers. Her mind began to swim with erotic thoughts about this seductive stranger and she felt him part her lips with his tongue and pull her closer to him.

As soon as his tongue met hers, strange sensation filled her body, as if every nerve had come alive with lust, and it was accompanied by a taste of something unfamiliar. Something sweet, but it gave her the idea of something deadly, like dark cherries mixed with a tempting poison. His lips held hers in place while their tongues circled each other's. She pulled back in wonder, still trying to make sense of her feelings and thoughts, and she felt herself shiver.

"Are you cold?" he asked.

She nodded numbly, entranced by what had just happened. She was both intrigued and frightened by this dark strange man looming over her like he wanted her as a meal.

"I, um, I have a jacket in the car," she said.

"Then let's go grab it," he smiled, leading her out by her hand. Clara allowed herself to be pulled back through the club, feeling something more than just the effects of alcohol. She felt warm and alive, and...desirous.

It was everything she could do not to pull this stranger in and dry hump him on the dance floor. She felt his hand on the skin of her back as he led her through a particularly crowded spot and she noticed herself leaning into him.

What the hell am I doing? Some sane part of her asked, but a louder part of her shut that up. An animalistic drive had awoken and it wanted her to rub herself against his body and pull him into her. She did her best to ignore that part too, and merely tried to walk. Soon she found herself in the parking lot with this man, facing Jahi's red Ferrari that she didn't have the keys to.

"Don't worry, I think I have a jacket in my car," he offered, guiding her over to a blacked-out SUV in the darkest corner of the parking lot. "Let's go see if I brought it."

He ran his fingertips sensually up her bare back. Now the sane side of her was screaming not to follow him to that shadowed vehicle, while the other part was imagining what else he could do with his fingers. She felt her feet moving in the direction of the SUV. In her drunken state her eyes wouldn't focus on anything for more than a split second, but he held her hand, ensuring she didn't fall.

Just as she turned the corner of the SUV she heard Jahi's voice behind her. "Clara no!" Jahi was running in her direction. "Tanus leave her alone!" Jahi's voice was loud with fear and the pitch rang with desperation. Clara pulled away, warned by the tension in Jahi's voice, but was quickly yanked under the man's arm forcibly as he fumbled to open the door to the SUV.

Jahi rounded the corner with a knife drawn. "Leave her alone Philotanus."

"Ah, come on Jahi, we could share her." He raised an eyebrow at Jahi and licked his lips. "We used to have a lot of fun together." He pushed Clara against the vehicle and kissed her roughly. Clara brought her arms up between them, not sure whether to pull him in closer or push him away.

Something isn't right.

"No. Let her go," Jahi said sternly.

The man stilled, then turned his head and studied Jahi. "So the rumors are true then? You've switched sides. Too bad, I'm going to miss the good times." He kissed Clara on the cheek, then opened the passenger side door. "Sorry though, this is a commissioned job. Nothing personal."

"No," Clara managed. "I want to go with Jahi."

She felt the man pushing her toward the open door of the vehicle, and finally was able to let the saner side take over her body, emboldened by the fear she saw on Jahi's face.

She spun herself away, striking him in the stomach with an elbow, then turned to face him, clapping both hands over his ears as fast as she could, rupturing his ear drums. Lines of tension formed on his face that wrinkled with pain as he clasped his hands to his ears. With his momentary pause, she stepped away and brought her knee into his groin as fast and hard as possible. He fell to the ground clutching his crotch and Clara ran for Jahi.

The girls sprinted to Jahi's car as fast as their heels allowed and leapt in when Jahi unlocked the doors. The engine came to life and Jahi backed out of the parking lot, just in time for them to see Philotanus emerging from the shadows. His eyes had turned to a terrifying black. Jahi shifted into drive and took off with a screech from her reluctant tires, narrowly missing some humans who dove out of the way of the car.

"Here," she tossed her purse at Clara. "Call Michael for me. We can't go home in case we're being followed." Clara did as she was instructed, and relayed all the messages between the two, while managing somehow to remain in the seat. Jahi drove the streets at a terrifying pace that caused Clara to pinch her eyes closed and wonder if there were any more seat belts she could wrap around herself.

I'm not sure dying in a car crash is better than going with a sexy demon.

Within a few moments, Jahi pulled up to a cemetery off Santa Monica boulevard. Clara cringed when she saw that Ramatel had accompanied Michael and that his pissed off expression was directed at her. At least part of her cringed, the other side was excited to see him.

Jahi parked on the side of the road and ran into Michael's arms, explaining the situation hurriedly. Clara was slower to approach. The effects of the alcohol, which she was beginning to think was some kind of demonic aphrodisiac, and the daunting look Ramatel was giving her caused her to slow her steps.

Despite this, she couldn't stop herself from scanning his body as she approached. His carved muscles were pulsing as he clenched and unclenched his fists, listening to the story Jahi was telling. The angry set to his jaw also made those lush lips stick out a little further. The hint of danger in his eyes was exciting to her.

Shadows on his face accentuated his features and his scars, and the glare he shot Clara could, with a little imagination, be passion. All the anger he was giving off screamed about the power from his body. *What would it be like to give into that power, to feel that power in her body? To taste it?* She licked her lips at the thought. *Yup, definitely an aphrodisiac* the sane part of her said. The other part decided to claim him tonight.

Chapter Eight

Ramatel felt his breath catch in his throat the
moment Clara had emerged from the car. He'd never seen
her so dolled up, but he forced himself to look away lest he
lose control and tackle her to ground right there. The
makeup darkened her eyelashes while the clothing
revealed a body that sent his pulse rate spiraling. He was
clenching and unclenching his hands in an attempt to stop
them from pulling her into him and stroking all that
available skin.

"Take them home, I'm going after Philotanus!"
Michael barked at Ramatel then disappeared before
Ramatel could offer to switch places. The last thing he
needed was to be stuck with babysitting duty, especially
when his self-control was waning. But then again, Michael
would never let a threat to his woman go unpunished.
Ramatel almost felt sorry for Philotanus.

Almost.

Ramatel cursed at the empty spot where Michael had
been, then turned to Jahi. "Can you get home?"

She nodded.

"We'll come back for your car tomorrow."

Jahi looked around her to ensure no one was
watching them, then she disappeared.

Ramatel reached for Clara's arm and pulled her
close to him. "Come here."

She wobbled into him and put her hands around his
arm to stop herself from falling. As soon as she had a good
grip on his bicep, Ramatel disappeared with her, only to
reappear back the room they shared.

"Stay here, I'm going to go make sure Jahi made it home."

"Are you coming back?" she asked, her drunken eyes going wide. *She's probably scared to be alone,* he presumed. She had just had her first demon encounter after all, and she had to suffer Jahi's driving.

"Yes." Ramatel left her and headed for the main house. Jahi was in her room and she assured him that she was fine. He let her know that the kids were with Gabriel learning to process a scene and reminded her to find him if she needed to leave at all.

"You two have fun," she called teasingly after him.

What does that mean? Ramatel returned to his room and, for once, he knocked on his own door, not really sure what condition he would find her in. *She could be crying. Girls do that when they are scared. Or she might be vomiting, she was pretty drunk after all.*

"Come in," Clara called.

Well she sounds okay. With a quick turn of the door knob he walked in only to find Clara facing him. She leaned against the desk wearing a black lace bra that pushed her pert breasts together, a tiny lace thong barely covering anything, and a garter belt holding up fishnet stockings. Her hair was loose and fell over her freckled shoulders. Her pale skin seemed to reflect the moonlight from the window, and those green eyes were locked on him.

His cock immediately became interested just as the rest of him became frightened. He wanted her in the worst way, and she was drunk. There had to be rules against this. Even if there weren't she would regret this tomorrow when she sobered up to his scarred flesh.

"What the hell are you doing?" he demanded. Immediately pissed off to be tempted with something he knew he couldn't have. "How much did you drink?"

She straightened her back and ignored his questions. "Come here Ramatel." She raised a hand to her chest and let it slowly glide down until she cupped her own breast, and moved her thumb back and forth across the barely hidden nipple.

Heat erupted from his loins causing him to suck in a long breath. *Be strong.* He folded his arms across his chest as if to put up a barrier, then swallowed hard and backed up. Then the realization occurred to him, she'd been with Philotanus, demon of seduction. "Did you kiss him?"

The look of guilt was all he needed for an answer. "Dammit Clara! He's poisoned you with an aphrodisiac!" The image of her kissing him flashed into his mind, and the rage began to boil beneath his skin.

A demon dared to touch my chinfon! MY chinfon. Ramatel made a silent vow to hunt Philotanus down and punish him if Michael didn't kill him tonight.

Clara's advance paused with Ramatel's change in expression. "Oooh, you're mad, aren't you?" she asked in a teasing, sing song tone. "Are you going to spank me again?" She turned around, and bent slightly over the desk, tempting him with the bare round ass he wanted to grip already.

Ramatel's feet carried him over to her, as if by their own command. Even his own body was turning against him. He did want to spank her. He wanted to punish her for letting any other man touch her at all. He wanted her to know who commanded her body, and it was him.

Slap! His hand connected with the bare skin. The flesh of her backside rippled with the pressure while her body tensed.

Slap! He brought his hand down on the other cheek, and this time she yelped. *Yes! He was in control!*

Slap! Her cheeks were revealing bright red hand prints against her pale white skin. *My mark. Mine!*

Slap! This time she arched her back causing her round little ass to stick out even more, but he left his hand there, feeling the warmth of the skin beneath it. It had to feel like it was burning her, but he let it sit while his eyes explored her back.

Even here freckles abounded, but the muscles were visible from her training and whatever she did in her former life. That narrow waist gave her an hourglass shape, complementing the round tight ass and curvy legs. His hand slid up and began roaming freely over her back. He looked down and saw his scarred hand touching her delicate skin and reality hit him.

No! She's drunk and drugged. I can't take advantage of her, and I can't have her.

He turned to flee the room, not trusting himself to even try to apologize this time, but she chased after him and leapt in front of him before he reached the door. He stopped short, feeling her breath on his chest. She pushed her lips up to meet his while she threw her arms around his neck and pulled him into her.

It felt so good to be touching her. He felt something awaken in him that he was sure had died in hell, and he put his arms around her waist, pulling her against him while his tongue spread her lips and entangled itself. He wanted more of him in her than his tongue. He wanted to touch her everywhere and feel her skin against his. He wanted...

No!

He pulled back again. "No!" he tried to sidestep around her but she moved, blocking him with her body and pulling him in for another kiss. This time he felt her palm against his shaft through his utility pants, and he pushed into her hand instinctively. The warm sensations as she tightened slightly almost made him come on the spot.

I have to fight this.

One more failed attempt to leave, left him with what might have been his only option. She was not going to take "No" for an answer in her drugged state, and he didn't know how long the effects would last.

He let her kiss him again, and fought the urge to use his hand to tighten hers further around his shaft. Instead, he reached for the rope that held the sheet/wall to her room and gave it a sharp tug, whipping it to free it from the sheet with a snap. He flashed them over to his bed area and in a few seconds he'd wrapped the rope around her wrists.

She cried out in surprise and tried to sit up but he pushed her back onto the bed and made fast use of the rope to lift her arms to the headboard where he tied them, using his weight to pin her while he worked.

"There," he gave what he knew was a satisfied smile and rolled off her to the side. She pouted and stuck her bottom lip out. Damn, he wanted to nip at that lip. "We can't do this. You'll regret it tomorrow, I promise. It's just the drug making you act like this."

She shook her head. "Uh uh. Can I tell you a secret?" She lifted her head off the pillow and brought her mouth close to his ear. "I want you when I'm sober too. I watch you when you work out…" she tongued his earlobe sending shivers down his body, "…and when you undress."

He turned to face her to see if she was being serious. Her face was all earnest and she held his gaze. Ramatel felt himself moving to kiss her and he pushed his lips roughly, desperately, against her. "You can't mean that, but I wish it were true," he said against her mouth.

"It is true. I've wanted you since that first night," she said when she could get away from his mouth for long enough.

He stopped kissing her and lifted his head, staring down into her green eyes.

Be strong. "Even so, my last relationship landed me in hell." He pushed himself up to his knees and began to make his way to the edge of the bed.

"Wait! You would leave me here like this? Please, Ramatel, I need a release. Please?"

He froze and looked down at her again. He knew Philotanus's drug was potent, and probably was made worse with the alcohol. She probably wasn't exaggerating. She would hurt if she didn't get it. *Surely the Father couldn't object to me helping her.*

***

Clara felt urges in her body in a way that she never had before. There was a necessity to be filled, to feel skin, to lick, and touch and grind. She felt she would come apart from the inside if she didn't get laid and the object of her affection was right in front of her about to walk away.

"Please Ramatel?" she begged, sliding her legs up the sheets to trap him between them.

His face softened as he studied her, then to her relief, he moved in to kiss her. When his lips were on hers she pressed her breasts into his chests and fully locked her legs around him.

"Fine," he agreed. "But no sex."

She made a pleading whimper but he caught her lips again and kissed her so deeply her reality muddled. Their tongues explored each other, gliding across the other's as they breathed the same air. She felt his hands on her ribcage climbing their way up to cup her breasts. She was so sensitive that at first she startled at the touch then pushed up to offer more. He flicked his thumb over her peaks causing her eyes to widen and her breath to catch on its way out of her chest. He noticed her reaction and did it again, smiling down at her as he teased.

"Why?" she finally asked, causing him to pause. "Why no sex?" she pushed herself against his crotch when she asked. He let out a frustrated breath and shook his head, which she understood to mean "no discussions."

She felt his hands fumbling with the clasp on the front of the bra, then it sprung free. Instead of latching on, he gently pulled the material to the side. He studied her for an achingly long moment before kissing one breast, just to flick her hardened nipple with his tongue.

"Ramatel please, more."

He smiled up at her eyes from her chest. "Yes, but my way. My rules." He flicked her nipple with his tongue again, then put his lips around it, pulling her into his mouth. The sensation on her skin caused her to buck wildly. She felt him caress her with his tongue in circles and strokes, while his other hand cupped and stroked on the other side. With a long final draw, he pulled back from her pink flesh and moved to the other nipple, repeating the treatment until she was writhing beneath him.

He sat back, unhooking her legs from him and began to slowly and deliberately unhook her garter from her stockings. He rolled each stocking down her leg, and slid his hands up her legs as if to work on her thong. He didn't begin on that immediately though.

First, his hands clamped on her hips and he bent forward to place an exquisite, simple kiss over her lacey thong, eliciting a pleading whimper from her. He breathed in deeply and she saw the corners of his mouth turn up in an appreciative smile. He stayed there a long moment and she didn't dare to move lest she ruin the moment. The look on his face told her he was savoring something. He had closed his eyes, but still held the same smile.

Finally, he opened his eyes again and struck out with a long stroke of his tongue over her thong. Her mouth fell open when he did and she furled her eyebrows in an imploring manner. In her head she commanded him to do it again.

He smiled fully now, revealing perfect white teeth, and hooked his fingers into the side of her underwear, tugging them down. She lifted herself to assist and he moved from between her legs until he'd pulled them down. These he folded into a neat little triangle and placed them under the unused pillow on the king bed.

"Mine," he whispered.

She nodded up at him. He lay beside her now, caressing her skin with the backs of his fingers. Deliberately avoiding the areas she most wanted to feel his touch.

"You're teasing me," she whispered.

He nodded. "You've teased me with that body for a week now." He lifted one of her knees and rolled her slightly onto her side as if he intended to spoon her, but instead he slapped her butt again then pulled her into him. "And I'm not a nice angel."

She smiled to herself and wiggled her butt against his shaft, glorying in the breath she felt him suck in when she made contact. His hand moved over her stomach from her hip then down toward to sex. She opened her legs for him. She felt him part her folds, with slow smooth strokes, over and over, until she was wriggling, trying to push herself onto them. He held her at bay, but rolled her onto her back again.

He brought his hand back to his mouth and wetted his thumb, only to return his hand and seek out her clitoris. He knew immediately when he'd found it because her sensitivity made her jump. He used slow motions to stroke her, until she was gasping for air. She tried to roll into him, begging him to let her come.

"Still," he ordered her, but then his expression softened again. "It has been a long time since I've known a woman. Let me enjoy this too," he whispered.

She nodded and then felt a finger probing at her entrance. One slipped in, bringing a moan from her lips. She thought she might come just from that, but it retreated, then pushed in again. His thumb made its way back to her most sensitive spot and made tiny strokes, matching the movement of his finger inside her. She felt the pleasure building fast and let him know with low, guttural noises that she was helpless to contain.

Finally, she couldn't hold out any longer and she felt her sex grip his finger as she pushed against his thumb.

She unsuccessfully tried to hush a scream as her muscles tensed throughout her body. He stilled his hand and watched her intently until she relaxed. When she opened her eyes he was smiling down at her with a look of accomplishment.

She returned his smile, but her body wasn't completely satisfied yet. "More?" she asked.

He bent to kiss her mouth, then moved to whisper in her ear. "Yes, much more."

She felt him insert another finger into her and she tried to drive herself against him. He pulled his wrist back and pushed it forward until she was moaning into his neck. This went on until she felt herself tensing again, then he expertly hooked his fingers and caressed a pleasurable spot, sending her into another climax immediately.

Again he studied her reaction with a self-satisfied expression, but he pulled his hand away from her, leaving her feeling empty. She tried to roll his way again, but he pushed her back, and scooted down the bed until he knelt between her legs. Hope flared in her, thinking she might have won out and that he would finally, fully fill her with himself. But when he bent his head forward, she learned she was wrong.

At first his mouth hovered over her glistening sex, occasionally sending out a darting tongue to tease. He couldn't know that her blood felt like liquid fire already and that the teasing only raised the temperature more, or did he? She looked at him and he gave her an evil grin as his tongue darted out again. She tried to move her hips toward him, chasing his tongue, but he pulled away when she did. She heard a low chuckle.

"That's what you get for kissing another man." His tongue shifted its target and began to strike at her swollen clitoris now, causing her to make pleading noises each time. He struck out teasingly every time she felt herself begin to relax, causing her to tense again and await more teasing. She was hypersensitive to his touch, and he knew it. Finally, when she felt like she was going to fly to pieces, she begged.

"Please Ramatel."

He looked up and studied her as if he had to decide, then finally bent his head and licked at her folds. His tongue slid up and down tenderly until it pushed her way to her entrance. Her breath hitched in her chest and finally she was rewarded with a probing sensation as his tongue darted in and out. She felt herself moaning and begging as she received the pistoning of his wet tongue.

He replaced his tongue inside her with his fingers again as his mouth sucked its way to her clitoris. He nipped gently with his teeth and pulled lovingly. She panted and tried to muffle her cries into her own shoulder. At last, he sucked her into his mouth and curved his fingers up causing her to scream with pleasure as her body tensed. He sucked through her orgasm, giving her only a small moment to catch her breath before he resumed the same treatment and coaxed two more out of her in quick succession.

When Clara's panting had finally subsided, Ramatel climbed up to lay his broad shoulders next to hers. Neither of them spoke, although she turned to him. He was staring her down intently, in a way she had never seen before. He looked at her with longing and something else…

Sadness.

She rolled in his direction to face him. "Please don't be sorry for what we did," she whispered.

He shook his head, and his lips curved into a placating smile. "I'm not."

"You look sad," she said softly.

His expression changed the moment she identified the emotion. He pinched his lips and rolled over as if now irritated. He sat up and began to leave the bed, without untying her.

"Did I do something wrong?" she asked.

"No." He disappeared.

Fucken moody!

Clara was left feeling shut out and rejected. She lay there naked, bared, and restrained, which was appropriate because that was exactly how she felt on the inside too. She replayed everything, trying to determine where things had gone wrong until eventually sleep lulled her into numbness.

Sometime later in the night, she felt the mattress depress under a lot of weight. In her groggy, drunken, and drugged state she still knew that Ramatel had returned and untied her arms. Her exhaustion from their exertion and the impending hangover, prevented her from fully awakening, but she felt him lower her hands and pull her into his powerful body in an embrace.

Clara might have heard him whisper "I'm sorry," but she wasn't sure whether it was real or if she dreamt it. Later when she woke up alone, she wasn't really sure about any of it, other than that she was no longer tied to the bed.

Chapter Nine

Late in the morning when Clara could drag herself out of bed, she showered, dressed, and crossed the lawn to the main house. Breakfast was asking too much from her stomach so she headed for Jahi's room.

She wasn't sure who she hoped to find there, Jahi or Michael. Part of her wanted to talk to Jahi, and part of her wanted everything to be normal and for Michael to lead her to the gym and assign a workout. She got Jahi.

"How did it go last night?" Jahi asked opening the door and beckoning her into the room with a knowing smile.

"Um, I don't... know." Clara said hesitantly. She looked around to verify that they were alone. She wasn't really sure if talking about this with Jahi was the right thing, but who else did she have? She ended up spilling to Jahi what had happened, leaving out a lot descriptive details.

"Wow!" Jahi said when Clara had finished her story. "Wild ride!"

"Are *chin-whatevers* allowed to date?"

Jahi shrugged. "I'm kinda new to this side of things. I can ask, but everyone will know who I'm talking about."

"Nah, that's okay." Clara declined. "I'll figure this out."

"Whahhhhahhhh," came a horrible sound from down the hall, startling them.

"What the hell is that?"

Jahi gave her a curious look in reply. "It sounds like a baby, but why would there be a baby here?"

The two of them left Jahi's room and followed the sound to Liwet's room. When they knocked and received permission to enter they found the large man, holding a tiny bundle of noise.

***

That night Gabriel called a meeting. Clara and Jahi had spent the day helping Liwet with the baby as much as they could, which was very little since neither of them knew anything about babies. Then again, neither did he. They joined the meeting and sat together in Gabriel's office. None of the other *chinfons* were there and compared to everyone else in the room Clara felt miniscule.

Gabriel sat on his desk looking exhausted. Asael and Barakel stood as close to the door as they could manage, while Michael lounged next to Jahi. The three "kids" sat anxiously in the chairs and loveseats of the sitting area with Liwet listening intently for signs of distress from the baby.

Clara looked expectantly for Ramatel, who was the last to arrive. He pointedly looked in every direction but hers before joining the other two fallen angels in their foreboding stances near the door. Clara felt Jahi look at her, but she decided to study the design on the carpet.

Gabriel began by asking Asael to explain what they found, and Liwet clicked through pictures of the evidence from the scene on a computer screen that everyone tried to gather around. Asael checked his watch a couple while Liwet was talking.

Clara was acutely aware of Ramatel's presence as he looked at the images, and was disappointed every time he asked a question because she took that to mean he was actually paying attention to the pictures and not to her. The images showed that the demons had been living out of the containers. There were sleeping bags, weapons, personal items, like MP3 players, cell phones, laptops, spare clothes, bags of flour and grain, a dog leash, and a baby crib.

"What do you make of it?" Michael asked Gabriel.

"I'm not sure. Butator can you go through the computers and phones and see what kind of intel you can pull?" The red-haired man nodded, not meeting Gabriel's eyes. "Hamal can you search the child abduction website for a baby? See if there are any amber alerts."

"I already did that," Liwet spoke up. "There was nothing."

"That website would only cover American abductions right?" Jahi asked. "That kid could be from anywhere."

"Right, that's why it's still here. If we give it to the authorities they will limit their search to one or two countries."

"She," Liwet said, drawing everyone's attention. "She's a girl."

Gabriel gave him a curious look but moved on. "Julie says *she* is about 6 months old, and it doesn't look like the demons had her for very long There was no formula or signs of an extended stay in the containers and she is healthy, so where ever she came from it was recently."

"I'll search all the human law enforcement websites around the world," Butator said.

Michael fisted his hair in frustration, then stood up and began to pace. "There are a lot of third world countries that don't have websites."

"The blankets and crib seem to be first world, but they could have gotten those thing here," someone spoke.

"Not likely if they weren't planning an extended stay," said another.

"We'll look anyway," Gabriel said, halting that discussion. "I've visited a lot of lesser angels today..." *That explained the exhaustion.* "...and put the word out for them to disseminate so if any of the angels hears anything it'll get back to me."

"If they weren't planning an extended stay then whatever they were going to do, they were going to do it quickly," Barakel added quietly.

"Yes," Gabriel agreed, "and that is the real question, isn't it? Any ideas on that?" The room went silent.

"Could they have just recently gotten the baby and not had time to get supplies yet?" Clara asked hopefully.

Gabriel shrugged. "Maybe, but demons aren't really the adoption type."

"Was the whole horde killed?" Michael asked.

Asael nodded.

"Well then let's move on." Gabriel said, guiding the discussion. "Something else happened last night. Jahi, Clara, care to elaborate?"

Isn't that an understatement. Clara ducked her head, wanting to avoid speaking in case she gave away something by accident. Fortunately, Jahi took over the story telling.

"...You shoulda seen my girl here," Jahi said patting Clara's arm toward the end of her story. "She's got moves on and off the dance floor!" Clara blushed but Jahi continued. "When she heard he was a demon, she beat Philotanus like he was a schoolboy and we took off. That's when we called Michael."

Blessedly, Jahi had left out the part about her kissing the demon and everything else that followed that night. Clara tried to eye Ramatel and caught Asael checking his watch again.

"Do you think you were targeted specifically or did he just get lucky?" Gabriel asked of them. They both shook their heads that they didn't know.

"He'd been watching us since we got there. I never saw him looking at anyone else," Clara mentioned.

"He was there when we got there?" Jahi asked.

Clara nodded. "We walked past him in line."

Jahi raised an eyebrow and shot her a smile to suggest Clara had been checking out the demon.

"Hey, I was just being aware of my surroundings," Clara said defensively. "He also said it was a commissioned job."

"Don't suppose he said for whom?" Michael asked. Clara shook her head.

"You think these two things were related?" Hamal, black "kid" asked.

"Could be, I have no idea," Gabriel answered. "Was he with anyone?"

"He was talking to someone in line, I don't know if he was with them or not. I never saw him with that guy in the club." There was a long pause in the conversation while everyone seemed to be deep in thought.

"The only other time you've left the estate was with shopping with Jahi, right? Did you see him there?" Asael asked. She shook her head.

"Ok, so Philotanus is trolling for women. If some demon wanted a woman, why not go get her themselves?" asked Liwet.

"The commissioner may not be topside." Jahi answered. "But the fact that they commissioned him means that they either want someone willing or that their plans involve something sexual. Philotanus doesn't come cheap either. The commissioner would be a heavy hitter."

"I don't suppose you have any friendly old acquaintances you could ask?" Gabriel said to Jahi. She gave him a doubtful look, but offered to try.

"I'm going with you." Michael said sternly. Jahi just nodded.

"If these two things are related," Michael said, seeming to be putting the thoughts together as he was speaking them, "catching Philotanus or any associates he has might lead to some information."

Gabriel nodded. "Whether he was after Clara or any random human, Philotanus might still be out looking for women, or men for that matter. Clara, how would you feel about joining the search? Lure him out?"

Clara nodded and saw Asael and Barakel smirking at Ramatel who did not look pleased.

"It's too dangerous for her!" Ramatel quipped sternly.

"That's why you'll be with her. I'll adjust the duty schedule accordingly."

"Might give you two some QT," Asael teased Ramatel with a glint in his eyes.

"Like living together isn't enough?" Ramatel mumbled sullenly.

"Apparently not," Gabriel added, then his attention turned to Liwet. "May I have a word with you?"

Evidently that was some indication that the meeting was adjourned and everyone began to make their way out the door. Everyone but Liwet.

Chapter Ten

Liwet watched everyone else exit Gabriel's office, but he was actually listening to make sure he didn't hear sounds from the baby. Fortunately, she was sleeping now that she had finally drained a full bottle of formula. He'd taken to calling her Sarah, just as a way to think of her until they got her back to her rightful home.

"Sorry you got strapped with baby duty," Gabriel's voice called his attention.

"Eh, she's not that bad... when she's sleeping," Liwet laughed.

"The Carmelite Sisters have agreed to watch the ba-"

"I can do it," Liwet insisted. He felt Gabriel studying him, probably thinking of every reason he shouldn't be the one to watch her. Liwet grew twitchy, waiting for the arguments. He didn't really want to give up the baby though. Sure, he would to her parents, but not to other strangers who hadn't just spent that last 12 hours feeding her, pacing the floor to get her to sleep, changing her, watching over her. They would just be strangers to her. He'd already figured out that she liked one brand of formula over the others and that Pampers fit just right but Huggies fell off, even though they were the same size. *No, he would be taking care of her, at least until they found her parents.* Liwet finally met Gabriel's eyes in a challenge.

The challenge he expected wasn't there though. Gabriel just looked exhausted. "Alright, thank you," Gabriel said turning away.

"Gabriel?" Liwet asked. "You alright."

Gabriel scrubbed his hand over his face. "Yes I'm fine. I'll let you know if we find anything on her parents."

***

Ramatel, Asael, and Barakel all headed to the back house in silence. Asael walked quickly ahead of the others and let himself in.

"You're in a hurry," Ramatel noted when they'd caught up. "Big date?"

Asael smirked. "Maybe. I'm a popular guy."

Ramatel snorted. "I bet. I hear there is even a waitlist for your… dates."

Asael grinned this time, making the fang piercings stick out a little. "What can I say, ladies love the Viper."

"I wouldn't call them ladies."

"Don't hate, we don't all get hot little *chinfons* to occupy us."

"Lucky you…" Ramatel grumbled.

"Hey, if you don't want her…"

Ramatel jabbed a punch at Asael's face. Asael blocked it but didn't fire any back. "Save your energy brother, she's not my type."

"Too female?" Ramatel joked.

"Too headstrong," Asael replied seriously. "You can have that shit."

Ramatel calmed himself and stepped back, just as Clara walked in, carrying a tiny black dress on a hanger that she'd borrowed from Jahi. She looked startled to see them all stop and look at her, as though she knew she was interrupting something. She nodded to them, then headed toward the room she shared.

"I think she likes you," Asael commented.

"That's the problem," Ramatel grumbled and pinched his lips together.

"What do you mean?"

Ramatel shot him a look of consternation. "You and I both know that guys like us don't get happily ever after."

Asael sighed and nodded then dropped his gaze to the floor. He rubbed his wrists as though they were sore but seemed lost in a memory. "Yeah. I know it."

Ramatel left Asael to whatever engagement he had for the night. Both Ramatel and Barakel were aware of Asael's proclivities, but hey, to each their own, right? Ramatel walked into his room, straight to his sectioned-off half, trying not to imagine Clara changing on the other side of the room. He strapped his knives into his belt, checked his pocket for his backup weapon, and then sat down on the bed to wait for her. He heard her tiptoeing past his sheeted wall to the bathroom and turned to see her in a tiny black dress that revealed her curvy legs and clung to her form.

He had to turn away before he ripped it off her and tackled her to the floor. Eventually he got bored waiting for her to get ready and lay down on his covers. His sheets still smelled like her. He breathed deeply, then remembered that he'd kept a souvenir of that smell. His fingers searched under a pillow and grasp the lace. He smiled thinking about the orgasms he'd given her. She was so responsive. He wondered if she was always like that or if that was Philotanus's work.

He sat up and peered into the bathroom. The door was open and she was applying makeup she didn't need. The tightness of her dress against her narrow waist only served to make her round hips and butt appear even more delectable. He envisioned her dancing in a club and knew that she was going to draw a lot of attention. His teeth clenched at the thought of men looking at her body like that. He fumed about it, and what he would do to any man who ogled her, until he found a loophole in Gabriel's plan.

He walked to the bathroom door and tried not to reveal the urge to pull the dress up and take her against the sink. "Go change your clothes." She gave him a look with raised eyebrows that indicated she did not like to be ordered around. "I have an idea." He offered as an explanation, then stood aside to let her out.

He wasn't sure if she was going to listen to him or not, but she did put her brush down and push past him. He caught the smell of her shampoo as she passed, hoping she didn't notice him ducking his head to do so.

A short time later she emerged dressed similarly to him in black utility pants and a black long sleeved shirt.

"Better?" she asked.

He nodded. "Ready?"

"Yup."

He strode over and put an arm around her. She stepped closer and embraced him, pressing her breasts to his chests. Her eagerness put him on edge but he couldn't back away yet. He transported them to the roof of the nightclub she'd been in the night before, then stepped away from her embrace. After scoping out the area, he decided to move them across the street where they'd be able to see people who entered.

"A stakeout?" she asked as she set herself down beside him.

"Yes."

Chapter Eleven

They sat in silence for a long time, or actually about five minutes, which was as much silence as Clara could tolerate. She was sitting cross-legged watching the door of the club, but it was early and foot traffic was light. She'd been replaying the night before in her head all day, but he didn't seem to be dwelling on it at all.

"Can I ask you a question?"

Ramatel glanced at her from the corner of his eye. "You just did."

She sighed her frustration out and caught a hint of a smirk on his face. She lightly backhanded his arm. "You know what I mean."

He chuckled. "What's your question?"

"Last night… you were jealous that I'd kissed another man, but then you didn't want to have sex with me. I don't get it."

There was another long silence. She waited until she figured he'd had ample time to gather his thoughts. "Well?"

"Well what? That wasn't a question."

"Why?"

He pressed his lips together but never moved his eyes away from the door to the club. "I don't want to talk about it."

Clara decided to let the subject drop, for now. She'd seen the results of his mood swings and figured it was best not to tempt fate. She let another silence hang in the air for as long as she could stand it then interrupted it again.

"How old are you?"

The shifting of his eyes suggested that he was considering his answer for a while. "All in all, probably twenty-five hundred, maybe three thousand years. It's hard to tell. I think I stopped counting at twenty, unless you mean how old am I this time around, then I'm about one."

She ventured a glance at him and found the edge of his mouth curved into a slight smile.

"So that's what happened last night? You didn't want to be a cradle robber," she grinned at him, but he scowled back. "I'm surprised you even heard that. The big bang didn't blow out your ears?"

He nudged her with an elbow. "Smart ass."

"So what were the dinosaurs like?"

He chuckled a little again. "That was like six million years ago. I'm not *that* old."

She tried to watch the door to the club again, but her attention failed. "How long were you on earth before you went to hell?"

"What is this, twenty questions?" he grumbled.

She shrugged. "Sure."

"You must be halfway done by now then."

She laughed. "Nah, I'm just getting warmed up. Guess I'll need more than twenty," she gave him a teasing smile.

"Do I get a turn?" he asked, still staring at the door with a much better attention span than she had.

"Shoot," she replied.

"Do you really watch me undress?" he turned to look at her and she met his eyes.

"Yes," she replied, although she felt herself blushing as she said it.

"Why?"

She arched her eyebrows and smiled. "Because I like what I see."

This seemed to make him uncomfortable because he immediately broke eye contact and resumed staring at the door.

"Does it bother you?" she asked, afraid she had offended him.

"No." Another long pause, this time broken by him. "How do you know what you like, have you remembered who you were?"

"No," she said thoughtfully, "but I think I know what kind of person I am, even though I don't remember how I got this way. I know I don't like ketchup and that I can drive a car, but I don't remember who taught me to drive or the last time I had ketchup. It's like someone left the foundation but removed the house."

He nodded.

She resumed studying the door of the club and listening to beat of music coming from it. She wasn't really paying close attention though. She was still reflecting on the night before. It was like he had a split personality, part of him seemed to want her. She remembered the smile on him when he was smelling her, and he'd even kept her underwear! He didn't want her kissing other men, that was certain.

But then again, he also didn't want to have sex. He hadn't even removed his clothes. He wouldn't talk about why, and he usually seemed irritated by her presence. Was he ashamed of his scars? Maybe he did want sex. He said it had been a long time. Maybe he wanted sex but just didn't want her. Were there rules against it?

She was pulled out of her head when she saw him stiffen and lean closer to the edge.

"Is it him?" she whispered.

He shook his head. "No, just a demon crony."

"I don't think this is what Gabriel had in mind when he asked if I would help."

Ramatel lifted his shoulders in a quick shrug. "Gabriel isn't your *chinshen,* I am."

"What does *chinshen* mean?" she asked, tilting her head to watch him from the corner of her eye.

He thought a moment. "The closest thing in your language would be something like mentor or caretaker."

"What language is it?"

"Angelic."

"So lover isn't in the job description?" she asked, turning to watch his reaction to a question like that.

There was no answer, he didn't even glance in her direction. She gave up studying him and disappointedly resumed staring at the gray wall of the club below.

"I don't know. I've never had a *chinfon* before." She caught herself smiling and hope flared in her chest, until he continued talking. "But not with me Clara." He turned to face her. "I can't be your lover."

"Your behavior last night spoke a different story."

"I only did that for you because the poison would have hurt you if I didn't. I was doing you a favor. It won't happen again."

Clara felt her mouth fall open with the sting of rejection. He had just confirmed that her feelings were unreciprocated. All that time he spent avoiding her now made sense. He'd never wanted her in any way. Her

cheeks heated with humiliation and shame. She repeated
the words in her head. "Doing you a favor."

   She wanted to cry and punch him at the same time,
but she did neither. Instead she stood and stepped away
from him. She didn't want to be near him anymore. She
headed for the door to the stairs.

   "Where are you going?" he called after her.

   "Like you care. I'm just some kid you got strapped
with. I'm leaving."

   He appeared right in front of her before she reached
the door. "No."

   She couldn't have hated him more in that moment,
and she felt her body stiffen with anger. "Leave me alone.
I don't want a caretaker. I can take care of myself." She
stepped around him.

   "Like you did last night when you let a demon pull
you to his car? What would have happened if Jahi hadn't
been there?"

   "Shut up!" she screamed. "You don't get to act
concerned! You just admitted that you want nothing to do
with me!" She stormed past him and reached for the door
handle.

   "Clara, stop!" he commanded, and she froze. Not
voluntarily, but she did freeze. It felt like her body had
been encased in cement. He was forcing her to hold still.
He grabbed her wrist and her body broke free of its trap in
time to feel herself pulled back to the spot they had been
watching from. She tugged and hit and cursed at him as he
pulled.

   "Sit," he commanded with the same force he had
before and she felt her body comply. He sat next to her,

just as they had been a moment ago when they were joking around. Sitting as if everything was alright, but it wasn't.

She felt the hold release and heard him tell her to stay there. "We still have a job to do."

This wasn't a command but she sensed that if she tried to leave again he would make her stay. She felt angry tears welling up in her eyes and she turned away from him, hoping he wouldn't notice.

Chapter Twelve

Ramatel sat and listened to her sniffle. She hated him right now and she was right to. He'd hurt her, and taken away her free will, even if only for a moment. It was his right as her *chinshen* but it was also extremely frowned upon for obvious reasons, like the rift in the relationship. He'd led her on last night, then shut her out a moment ago. She wiped at her eyes. He hated that he'd hurt her.

"Clara… I'm sorry."

She stiffened and shivered. He pulled his jacket off, and meant to drape it over her until he saw the fat tears rolling down her cheeks. Then he reached out and hugged her from behind. "I'm sorry," he whispered again into her ear.

She began to sob outright and he turned her around so she sobbed into his shoulder. "I hate you right now," she squeaked.

"I know. I hate me too."

"Let me leave," she said when she managed to catch more air.

"No, I can't protect you if I'm not with you."

"What do you care if I get hurt? You just said you don't want me," she accused.

"No, I never said that." He hated that she thought that and needed to make sure she knew that wasn't why. He cupped her chin and brought her tear soaked face up to look at him. "I never said that I don't want you Clara. I do."

She stopped crying and chewed on her bottom lip as if trying to keep it still. "Then why Ramatel? Why not have me?"

This time he looked away. How could he tell her all of the things going through his mind? He wanted to tell her that anything good he let himself have would be taken away, if not outright destroyed by him. He wanted to say that he was afraid to be punished and go back to hell. He wanted to tell her that he didn't trust himself not to hurt her and that he wasn't good enough for her, but he couldn't bring those words to his mouth, not yet.

It felt as if saying them out loud would solidify his fears, or make her think him crazier than she already did. He knew he wasn't crazy though, all these things had already happened to him. They would happen again. What would she think of him then? She would be afraid of him. If he told her about the things that had happened in hell she would hate him. She'd be disgusted at his weakness. How could she not be? He was disgusted with himself.

He didn't answer her. He couldn't make his voice work. But he needed her to know that it wasn't because he didn't want her, so he kissed her. A deep, urgent kiss, as if he were trying to explain all of his thoughts with his lips and tongue. He finally pulled away, leaving her breathless.

"Ramatel, this is…" she drifted off as if to gather her thoughts. "I never know where I stand with you. One minute you act like you hate me and you're destroying the room, then you're kissing me. This is a rollercoaster."

"I know. I'm sorry." He stared at her and wished he could bring his mouth to voice all those crazy thoughts, but she wouldn't understand. How could he explain what two thousand years of hell had done to him?

A rollercoaster. That was apt. Welcome to my world, he thought. *Where emotional dysregulation seems to be the name of the game.*

***

"Wait, you mean he actually used *chinshen* commands on you?!" Jahi said incredulously. They were in the media room and preparing to watch a movie. Several days had gone by, and Clara and Ramatel had resorted to a distant professionalism. They talked about work and, occasionally, about light things, like what to pack for the stake outs, but never anything serious.

Clara had inferred, however, some changes that were positive. When she'd rubbed her knuckles bloody on the punching bag while training, Ramatel had noticed her hands that night and provided her with a pair of gloves the next day. Once she'd jolted awake in the middle of the night with images of the gun and the bright muzzle flash of the shot that killed her. Ramatel had awoken when she screamed and he'd given her a long, soothing hug, then laid her down and tucked her in. Nothing romantic had transpired though. Eventually, Clara decided to tell Jahi about their intimate encounter and see if she had any advice.

"Yeupp," Clara replied bitterly, still hostile at the memory of his control over her body. "He apologized for it, kissed me, and has barely spoken to me since."

"Woah, what the hell?" Jahi asked as she skimmed through the selection on the TV.

"I know, right!? Talk about mixed messages."

"Let me ask you something." Jahi sat up from her lounge. "Why him? You are obviously infatuated or else you wouldn't care. So why him?"

This time Clara didn't deny it. Instead, she wondered to herself about the answer. "I don't know. It

could be a lot of things. Maybe it's just 'cause he's hot…"
Jahi made a face indicating that she disagreed, but Clara
ignored her. "… and we had that wild night together—"

Jahi rolled her eyes. "If that's all it takes, then go get
laid and forget about Ramatel."

"No, it's more than that. I like the way he looks at
me. When he's not being an ass, that is. Like how he
noticed when I had scraped knuckles or when I have a
nightmare. I like the way he holds me. He makes me feel
special. And even if he is chauvinistic and antiquated
about protecting me, I guess I feel safe with him."

"What about safe from him?" Jahi bit out with a
grin. "You've only known him for a couple weeks and in
that time, he's spanked you, cut you, and tied you up.
Maybe you have Stockholm Syndrome," Jahi teased.

Clara laughed. "That's part of the attraction. The
wild ride."

"Well if you're set on this, then you need a plan."

"A plan?" Clara asked, reaching for the popcorn and
tossing some in her mouth.

"Yeah, a plan on how to seduce him."

"You don't think that's a little manipulative?"

"Phft, please. It's progressive. You can't simply wait
around for men to get their heads straight, you'll be
waiting forever. You have to take matters into your own
hands." Her attention switched back to the screen. "This
one?" she asked referring to the movie.

Clara shrugged her indifference to the movie. "What
do you have in mind?"

"I'm not sure yet, but I'll think of something." She
hit play and the movie *Cruel Intentions* began to flash
across the screen. Jahi liked to watch movies. She'd said it

was like research into the years she'd missed out on before
she rose from hell.

An hour and a half later, the credits began to roll and
Jahi reached for some of the last of the popcorn. "So here
is what we know for sure. A, he doesn't want you kissing
other men. B, he is responsive when you dress seductively.
C, he goes out of his way to avoid you when you could be
alone together privately, like right now. Let's presume
that's because he wants you." Jahi stood and started pacing
like she was scheming a plan to overtake Fort Knox.

"Some of that was him *doing me a favor*," she made
air quotes.

"Bullshit, don't listen to his words. Watch his
behavior. My therapist says all behavior is
communication."

"You have a therapist?"

Jahi nodded, but still seemed deep in thought. "All
the Beverly Hills housewives have one." She turned and
paced back. "I wonder if we can recreate those
circumstances?" Jahi said as if to herself, her gaze still
unfocused as she thought out loud.

"You want me to kiss that demon again?"

Jahi laughed. "Well that would probably work, but
we haven't been able to find him. No, maybe we could get
you dressed up and get you to flirt with someone.
Apparently that makes Ramatel jealous."

"I doubt that's going to happen sitting on rooftops."

"No, probably not..." Jahi continued to pace. "Don't
worry. I'll think of something. I wonder if I can come up
with a way to get him to talk to me."

"Should I be worried that an ex-demon is scheming
on my behalf?"

Jahi shot Clara an evil grin. "Absolutely. You know what? Why don't you try again tonight when you get home? The others will be out of the house for a while."

"He'll just push me away again, or spank me."

"Fifty-fifty chance of a good time then, right?" Jahi grinned.

"How about we wait and see how the night goes? He's kind of moody sometimes."

"Sometimes?" Jahi raised an eyebrow to emphasize the sarcasm.

Michael interrupted the girl talk when he walked in. He'd been sleeping until now following a long night hunting demons. Clara had heard that he also stopped a drive-by shooting. He greeted Jahi with an emphatic kiss, again making Clara wonder if she should leave the two of them alone together. When they managed to pull themselves away from each other, Michael looked at Clara.

"You ready? It's legs day, then I think you're ready to join the kids for hand-to-hand sparring."

Clara moaned loudly and stretched but got off the couch. "You mean I'm not going to save my soul by watching movies with Jahi?"

Michael embraced Jahi again. "Well, it worked for me, but I already knew how to fight."

Clara headed for the door with Michael as Jahi called "Go easy on my man today Clara."

Clara grinned and waved goodbye to her.

Chapter Thirteen

That night Clara and Ramatel returned from lurking in the dark on another rooftop, where they had been watching another nightclub from a list Jahi had provided of potential places to find Philotanus. Their nights now consisted of silently watching, with Ramatel brooding and Clara frustrated. But tonight Clara had decided she wasn't going to wait for his mood to lighten, the way it had been in when they'd joked around on the first night.

They went through their nightly routines, taking turns dressing and using the bathroom to brush their teeth and wash their faces. When they'd both retired to their respective "rooms," Clara waited about fifteen minutes, hoping that was enough time for Ramatel to begin to doze off. When she decided it was around the right time, she left her bed, stripped naked, and headed to Ramatel's bed.

In the dark she felt her way under the sheets and covers, sliding smoothly in beside him. He was lying on his back in the center of the bed, wearing only a pair of shorts. The shadows concealed most of his features, but she could make out the dark eyelashes and the harsh scars. He smelled of warm spice and masculinity. When she let the bulk of her weight rest fully on the mattress, he jumped away from her pinning himself to the wall that the bed was pushed up against.

"What are you doing?" he barked.

Undaunted, she slid closer. "I'm cold."

"Then put on a sweatshirt," he bit out.

Clara reached for his shoulders, and revealed her bare torso from beneath the covers. "That's not the kind of warmth I crave," she whispered, as she closed the distance between them. She pressed her lips to his. The contact was soft, but as she teased him with her lips, she opened his mouth with her tongue.

For a brief moment, he kissed her back, applying his own pressure to their locked lips. Ramatel wrapped one arm around the small of her back while his other hand reached for her breast. Just as he squeezed her nipple, something snapped in him, and he pushed her away from him onto the bed.

"Dammit, woman! I can't do this." He started to shuffle his way off the bed in an effort to leave the room. This time his face revealed something else. Was it anger? No, she was familiar with his anger. Fear? Certainly not of her. Wait, she knew that look on his face.

Hate.

The spurn on his face burned her deeper than any insult she'd endured. "Wait, Ramatel," she felt herself saying dispassionately. "I'll stop."

He paused his escape, and Clara felt her heart sagging with disappointment. "I'll go," she managed to say, trying to hold her dignity together through the rejection. She didn't look at him. That would have shattered the shell she was trying to hide under.

She left the bed and walked to her side of the room. She could feel him watching her, but she didn't care, apparently she didn't have anything he wanted anyway. She pulled a long shirt over her head, and stepped into a pair of panties.

She sat on the edge of her bed facing him, but she was looking at the floor with a distant gaze. A glimpse in that direction told her he hadn't moved.

An emotional pain radiated from her chest through the rest of her body. *This was it*, she thought. *I just played the highest card in my hand, and it wasn't enough. I've tried for two weeks, and had some good times, but it wasn't enough. I wasn't enough.*

"Tomorrow I'm going to ask Gabriel if he can ask the Father to reassign me," she said, her voice heavy with defeat. Then she turned away from him and curled herself into as tight a ball as she could manage. The shield of her arms and legs were going to have to be enough tonight because she had nothing else left. She took a deep breath trying to regulate her breathing so she wouldn't cry.

"Clara..." strong arms wrapped her, and her mattress depressed with his weight. "That is not what I want."

Clara flailed at his embrace. "No!" she screamed feeling rage boiling over like an explosion of scalding water. "Get away from me! Don't act like you want me! Don't act like you care!" She turned to face him with as much fight as she could muster. "You don't get to comfort me when you're the one hurting me! I'm done with that shit! I'm done with you!"

She gave him a final shove and he backed away looking at her as if she'd stabbed him, then he turned and left the room.

***

Ramatel was in the kitchen area, tearing through the cupboards and refrigerator looking for something harder than water to drink. The few bottles he found were empty.

What the hell, this place is never dry!

A knock at the front door drew his attention away. *What now?*

Jahi was waiting outside the door when he opened it. She was wearing a pair of yoga pants and a sweatshirt, and she had a bottle of whiskey in one hand and some kind of mixer in the other. *God bless her.*

"Hi, care to join me for a drink?"

Ramatel followed her outside and sat with her at a poolside table. He wondered why there were two cups there already, but decided that asking about the cups wasn't a good use of his brain power. He needed the drink she was offering.

He would have joined her for a drink any time. She was one of the few who had also spent a considerable amount of time in the pit, and there was an unspoken kinship between the hell survivors. If one of them needed a drink, they wouldn't have to drink alone if they didn't want to. Plus, she wasn't an angel, so she wasn't prone the sanctimonious crap he expected from the others.

She poured them each a drink before speaking. "So what's going on Ramatel?"

He cleared his throat. "What do you mean?"

"Well, your body is tense like you want a fight and the expression on your face gives the impression that you just lost one. What's up?"

Ramatel sighed. "Roommate spat."

Jahi nodded. "Look, I know Clara wants you, and I know you've been intimate without finishing the job. So what's the trouble?"

How does she...? Oh, right. They're friends. Ramatel eyed Jahi over. He was really weighing his options about what to say or not to say.

Jahi kicked him under the table. "Don't look at me like that. I've been your friend a lot longer than I've been hers. Now spill. What's the issue? Do you not want her?"

"Of course I want her! She's gorgeous, and strong, and she stands up to me, and…" he trailed off. "I want her more than anyone I've ever known."

"And what? You couldn't get it up?"

He glared at her. "That's not the issue."

"What is?"

Ramatel sipped his drink. "There's a lot of them," he preempted. "I don't know if *chin* are allowed to have that kind of relationship."

"So ask," Jahi said flatly.

"I did."

Jahi shot him an impressed look. "And?"

"Gabriel said I have to ask permission from the Father."

"So what are you waiting for?"

Ramatel scrubbed his face with his hands. "It's not that easy for me." There was a silence and he knew Jahi was waiting for more. "I vowed I'd never speak to Him again after He left us in that pit to rot! Even when He released us he left us scarred. I fucken hate Him Jahi."

"You won't break your vow for this?"

"What kind of man would I be if I did?"

"You tell me."

"A weak one!" he spat out. "My body might have been broken in hell but my spirit never was! I always kept my vows and I'm not about to start breaking them now."

Jahi looked up at the stars that were decorating the night sky. "So the definition of someone who is weak is someone who breaks their vows? I hate to know what you think of me then. Every day I vow I'm going to start exercising and every day I break it." She grinned at him.

Ramatel pinched his lips together. "It's not like that. You're different. Besides, you were a demon."

"Oh?" Jahi raised an eyebrow. "Dual standards? If I were in love with someone and a vow to myself might be the only thing stopping me from being with them, what would you tell me?"

Ramatel just snorted in reply.

"Ramatel when you made that vow did you know Clara?"

"Of course not."

"Did you think you'd meet someone like her?"

Ramatel sighed longingly and took a drink. "Never in my wildest dreams did I dare to believe I could meet someone like her."

"So the situation has changed from when you made that vow. You didn't have all the facts about the future. Would you have made it if you had known you'd have met Clara?"

Ramatel took another long drink and held it in his mouth a moment before swallowing. "I don't know."

"When you are presented with new circumstances, new information, new facts, and you don't incorporate those into your decision making, do you know what that makes you?"

Ramatel raised an eyebrow.

"An idiot! It makes you an idiot. You gotta be flexible with your decisions because the world is constantly changing. We don't live now like we did before we were cast in because the world has changed. There are new things now, new people. I know you're the angel of endurance, but sometimes strength comes from knowing when to give up on something that isn't working."

There was a long silence while Ramatel weighed the things Jahi said. "You are right, but the vow wasn't to myself. It was to Him. If I break it, He wins. Every damn moniker on my body is from some demon who broke me, but I've never broken that vow. God hasn't broken me yet and I'll be damned if he does now after seventy generations."

Jahi gave him an eye roll. "You idiot. You think that by upholding that vow you are winning? The only people you are hurting are yourself and Clara. The Father doesn't seem to be bothered at all by your vow."

"What if this was His plan to get me to break the vow?"

"So?"

"I can't forgive him Jahi."

"I'm not asking you to. Asking the Father to be with Clara doesn't equal forgiveness, although it might be the very beginning of fixing a broken relationship."

"Why should I break first? The Father is the one who should apologize!"

Now Jahi took a drink and pondered for a moment. "What if he did?"

"What do you mean?" Ramatel cut his eyes at her.

"What if the Father apologized. How would your life be different? What would change?"

Ramatel looked up at the sky again. "Everything," he said. "Everything because I would know he overreacted, and if he was sorry then it would mean that I mean something to him."

"And what would you do with knowledge?"

"I would... I'd... I'd be happy," Ramatel stammered out.

Jahi gave him a knowing nod. "I don't know God very well. I've only met Him once. But it sounds like you've put your happiness on hold waiting for an apology you might never get. What I do know is that you mean something to the rest of us, and you mean the world to Clara."

Ramatel fixed his eyes on the pool as he considered what Jahi was saying. Eventually he decided she was right about his vow. There was more though. "But if I go up there, I can't be sure of what is going to come out of my mouth. There is a good chance it won't be good and I'll just end up in the pit again."

Jahi nodded. "Surely you can bite your tongue for 2 minutes?"

"Maybe. Maybe not."

"Even if not, God is a big boy. I'm sure he can handle your anger. It might even be therapeutic for you to confront him."

"Or suicidal."

"Well, then let's practice what you'll say. We can practice it so many times that you will just blurt it out when you get there. You can even take one of the angels for support."

"Jahi I know you mean well, but your husband and Gabriel were the ones who bound me and cast me into the pit. I know that they didn't have a choice but they aren't on my list of hand holders either. Besides, there's more."

Jahi sipped her drink but didn't rush him.

"Even if I ask and I get permission, what kind of life would we have? What if something happens and I lose her or I drive her away? I'm pretty damn good at that. What if I hurt her? I'm not exactly boyfriend material. I eventually break everything I touch. What if she fulfills her duty and leaves? I'd be hurt all over again, hell, that may be His plan to keep tormenting me. I don't want to drag her through my punishment."

"Hmm," Jahi brought her glass to her lips while Ramatel refilled his. "That's a lot of 'what ifs.' What if none of that happens? What if you are so afraid that you might lose her someday, that you never get to be with her at all? That seems tragic to me since she loves you. You're so afraid that you *might* hurt her someday that you don't see you *are* hurting her now to prevent something that isn't a certainty."

"She loves me?"

"*That's* all you got out of what I just said?!" Jahi reached over and swatted him aside the head. "I don't think she could make it more clear if she wrote it on a card and handed it to you."

There was some silence again as they both sipped their drinks and studied the night sky. Ramatel broke the silence. "I think I really fucked things up tonight. Tomorrow, she is going to ask Gabriel to ask the Father if she can be reassigned."

"Yeah, it sounds like you fucked things up, so apologize before she gets to talk to Gabriel. If she is still bent on it then I'll talk to her." Jahi stood to head into the house. She downed the rest of her drink and eyed Ramatel before she left.

"Ramatel, I love you like a brother, so I want to be very clear about something."

He raised his chin and met her eye.

"You're being a stubborn ass. Knock that shit off."

Ramatel watched her walk away and even smiled at her last words. He headed back to his own place and quietly crept back into his room. Clara was still curled into a little ball on her bed. He pulled up the new desk chair that she had acquired, a metal folding chair, and sat facing her bed. He had a lot on his mind, and he was afraid that if he closed his eyes she would wake up and go find Gabriel then disappear. So he sat there and watched her while he poured over all of things Jahi had just said to him. *When did she get to be so smart?*

Ramatel sat for hours, listening to the hypnotic sound of the air filling her lungs and vacating it. He wanted to reach out and pet her hair, but he was afraid to wake her. He replayed the conversation over and over. First finding new arguments against what Jahi had said, then finally thinking through what she would say in reply to them. Eventually, he ran out of arguments and came to one very obvious conclusion... he was a stubborn ass.

Chapter Fourteen

Around eight that morning, Ramatel heard a knock on the bedroom door. He got up to answer it quickly before the caller had a chance to knock again and possibly wake Clara. Gabriel was on the other side of the door and Ramatel stepped outside of the room so they could speak.

"Sorry to bother you so early but there has been some information unlocked on those laptops that we recovered from the containers. Butator found a search for news headlines from the same area, a Mexican town called Nochixtlán, on two different computers. One specifically googled 'missing baby.' We think they might have been wondering if the baby's disappearance had become the center of attention or something like that." Ramatel listened intently, appreciating the news update but still wondering what this had to do with Gabriel knocking on his door. He really wanted to be there when Clara woke up so he could talk to her. Oh wait… Gabriel was still talking.

"… attacked the home of Armaita last night. She's fine, but Michael took Hamal there. I-"

"Sorry," Ramatel interrupted, wiping his tired eyes. "Who attacked whom?"

"At least two demons attacked the home of one of the local angel's houses."

Ramatel furled his eyebrows. "Another one? That's like three in the last year and a half, right?."

Gabriel nodded. "Brian hadn't made it to her house to put up the permanent wards. Anyway, since Asael and Barakel were in a fight last night, they're fine, killed five demons actually but Xaphan got away, but I was wondering if you would accompany me to Mexico?"

Ramatel's initial reaction was to protest, as he wanted to be here when Clara woke up, but then he realized that if Gabriel was away, Clara couldn't ask him to speak on her behalf to the Father.

Ramatel nodded. "Let me dress and leave Clara a note. I'll meet you outside in five."

Ramatel spent most of those few minutes trying to figure out what to write to Clara. Finally, he put his pen to the paper and wrote, "*Clara, I am sorry about last night. I had to go investigate something with Gabriel this morning, but can we talk when I get back? Please don't give up on me yet.*"

He met Gabriel outside and they disappeared. Ramatel found himself in front of a picturesque church that did not look like it belonged there. The ornate grey-stoned chapel housed a clock with two white bell steeples on either side. Gold domes umbrella'd the steeples and crosses sat atop each. Beside the church stood a building whose patio held five bright orange arches that contrasted sharply with the white of the building and the grey stone of the church. It was as if the people here were trying to upkeep the church and the surrounding buildings at the expense of the rest of the area, which looked about as run down as most Mexican towns.

Ramatel heard a frustrated sigh next to him. They were both cloaked so the humans had no idea they were being visited by angels.

"What is it?" Ramatel asked.

"It's a lot bigger than I'd hoped. I just wanted to ask the locals if any babies went missing lately, but with a town this size, they might not know. I wonder if it has a police station we could visit?"

"For information like that, you don't want a police station. You want a bar. Humans gossip a lot."

***

Clara had cried herself to sleep and did not rest well even when she had drifted off, so as if to compensate she slept well into the morning, and the early part of the afternoon too. Finally, when her body decided she'd had enough, she awoke. Ramatel was not there and the house was eerily quiet. Usually there were sounds of the "music" they listened to, which Clara knew now were metal bands with names like System of a Down, Five Finger Death Punch, Avenged Sevenfold, and Corn, spelled with a "K" and a backward R.

There was a note on the desk addressed to her and she read it, then re-read it. When she pulled herself together, she headed straight for Jahi's room.

"What do you think?" Clara asked. She had explained everything that happened the night before.

"Are you going to talk to him?" Jahi asked, ignoring Clara's question.

Clara pinched her lips together. "Yeah, probably. I don't know. Do you think if I do I'm being a doormat?"

"No, you are getting the information before you make a decision. If you don't like what he says then you still talk to Gabriel, you don't really have anything to lose."

"Unless it's some kind of manipulation. What if I just keep falling for this over and over and stay in an unhealthy relationship?"

"You don't even know what 'this' is. Just hear him out. It sounds like he might finally be ready to talk."

Clara continued to scowl.

"You know I'm right," Jahi continued. "Are you just trying to punish him for being an ass?"

Clara grimaced. *Was she that petty? Was she readable?* "Yeah, maybe."

"That kind of thinking isn't going to save your soul."

"Ok, fine." Clara was sick of being on the hot seat of scrutiny now. "Hey, where is everyone?"

Jahi filled her in on what she knew. Michael was off chasing two demons who had attacked an angel's house last night. Asael and Barakel had found and killed five lesser demons and were sleeping off the fatigue.

"That's really all I know, except that Gabriel had said that he wants another meeting tonight when everyone gets back."

With everyone off doing their own things, Clara and Jahi decided to make it a girl's day consisting of manicures and pedicures. They also helped Liwet out with the baby, which apparently Jahi had been doing daily. She'd become quite the diaper expert. Liwet looked exhausted so they brought Sarah into Jahi's room to give him a break.

Clara heard Asael and Barakel in the kitchen around three that afternoon, and Michael and Hamal were back by five. Clara kept listening for any signs of Ramatel and Gabriel. At some point she heard someone bring food to Butator, who was holed up in what Jahi had termed the computer cavern. Clara had glimpsed a work station there once with a least three laptops open, two large desk monitors, and a desk cluttered in books, papers, and all sorts of electronic components. Jahi usually tried to pull him out once a day but for the most part he kept to himself when he wasn't training.

Clara tried to make herself scarce to give Michael and Jahi some alone time so she found her way to the gym. Despite Jahi's suggestions and warnings, she wasn't exactly sure she wanted to give Ramatel another chance. There had been too many chances already. If he wanted to talk he would have by now. He'd had his chances while they were sitting in silence on rooftops.

Asael and Barakel had awoken and were in the gym lifting weights so Clara hopped on a treadmill. She lost herself in music she'd borrowed from the rest of the girls, and failed to notice that the men's weightlifting had led to weapons training until a wooden training knife went zipping past her head.

She looked over in shock and the two fallen angels mumbled apologies and gave her embarrassed looks. She waved the offense away and continued her run until she noticed that Barakel had the remaining knife and Asael was dodging and deflecting with ease. With a grin, Clara halted the treadmill and picked up the lost training knife from the floor, then began to creep up behind Asael. She knew Barakel saw her, but he didn't give her away by letting his eyes land directly on her.

When she was close enough, she pounced, pretending to stab the training knife into Asael's back where she would have hit a kidney had it been real.

"Ah! Wha-"

She kicked the back of his knee, forced him down to her level and held him in a choke while Barakel sliced and stabbed the training knife simulating a butchery, as Barakel laughed at the way they'd managed to fool Asael.

"No fair!" Asael bellowed, but though a grin.

"Knife fighting 101, always keep track of your weapons," Clara chimed through her triumphant grinning.

The door to the gym opened, drawing their attention, and Ramatel cleared his throat as though he felt he had interrupted something. He stared at Clara with an expression that seemed both relieved and fearful, maybe expectant. Finally, he managed to collect himself.

"Gabriel wants a meeting," he announced to everyone.

Chapter Fifteen

"So this is what we know…" Gabriel began, once everyone had arrived. Butator had unlocked some information on the laptops and Ramatel and Gabriel had followed a lead to investigate in Mexico. What they found was that there were about six babies missing, with their parents slaughtered, but they couldn't say with certainty that it had been demons.

"We may have found the home she was taken from," Gabriel said to Liwet, "and if we are right, she is, indeed, an orphan now."

Liwet hung his head and hid his expression from them. "I thought we decided she was a first world baby?"

"They must have acquired the crib and blankets here. There have been about five other babies missing from the local area too. The humans think it's some kind of cartel retaliation, and they could be right. The only evidence we have that demons were involved is the searches for missing babies in that specific region on demon computers."

"So demons are collecting babies," Hamal summed up.

"I found something else while you were gone," Butator added. He held up printed papers and handed them to Gabriel, then explained the contents to the others. "The demons were emailing some foreman or plant supervisor at the natural gas power plant in Long Beach. They kept asking about when alterations to one of the stacks would be complete. They wanted bronze plates lining the inside of the stack. The plant supervisor insists that it will be ready by the date requested."

"What date is that?"

"It doesn't say in the emails, and the only searches for anything I can find on the laptops are about summer solstice and sunset times."

Gabriel looked at the calendar and all the eyes in the room followed his. "That's five days away."

There was an eerie silence while everyone struggled to digest the new information.

Barakel's gruff voice broke in. "I'll say it. We're all thinking it. Molech. Their gonna use the plant to sacrifice babies." No one spoke to agree or to disagree.

"What's Molech?" Clara asked.

Gabriel answered her. "He was an ancient demon, worshipped as a Canaanite fertility god or sun god around 700 BC, give or take. He was depicted as a bull or a man with a bull's head." Michael got up and retrieved a book from the shelves lining the office while Gabriel spoke. "They used to have statues of him with seven chambers for sacrifices by fire. The bronze statue was a giant furnace."

"Like the stacks at a power plant," Barakel cut in.

Michael continued explaining. "Some of the chambers were for food, some for animals, and one for babies."

"They burned the babies!" Liwet cried in shock.

"Alive," Barakel added with a raspy voice. Michael handed Clara a book and the kids gathered around to read with her. There was an image of a huge statue with a bull's head and seven chambers in the chest. Below that was a large opening with a fire burning inside it. The hands of the statue were raised on either side.

"They also had orgies in front of the statue, which are described in the book of Leviticus, and now pigheaded humans try to use that to justify their homophobia because the demons didn't care if their victims were men or women. They think that by prohibiting worship of Molech the Father was prohibiting homosexuality. Fucken idiots! He was prohibiting child sacrifice."

"That would explain the leashes and the flour at the containers," Liwet said.

"And Xaphan the fire demon," Asael stated.

"And Philotanus's commission," Jahi added. "They probably want him to gather women for the orgy, and the purest make the best sacrifices. That's why he wanted Clara, she's washed clean. She reeks of virginity and innocence."

Clara felt her cheeks redden and Ramatel shifted uncomfortably in his chair.

"I smell?"

"Demons with sexually based powers can smell things like that. It's like being able to smell prey."

Asael chuckled from the corner. "Wonder what I smell like then?"

Jahi rolled her eyes "You don't want to know."

"Could this be linked to the attacks on angel homes?" Liwet asked, bring them back to the subject at hand.

Gabriel shrugged. "Maybe. They'd be a pure soul, but it would be a huge risk for the demons."

"Why would demons risk anything to sacrifice to another demon?" Clara asked.

"They're kind of like street gangs, and Molech is an OG, an original gangster. He's been in hell for almost three thousand years, but if he has enough souls saved up, he could commission jobs to get even more. Souls are currency there and with enough of them he could eventually buy his way topside. These demons are probably hoping to ride his shirt tails up or to make a little currency of their own by taking commissions," Jahi explained.

"So we have five days to figure out what to do," Gabriel pointed out.

***

Even by the end of the meeting Ramatel was still disturbed by the sights of the slaughtered families that he and Gabriel came across in Mexico. The demons had sliced and bled entire families, and only the best and most pure families of course, just to take the babies so they could burn them alive. It was one thing to see that kind of brutality in hell. It was another thing to witness it up here. It didn't belong here. It felt like a stain.

Then there was what he saw in the gym that Ramatel had to wrap his mind around too. Clara was laughing with Barakel and Asael. It was the first time he had seen his brothers smile since... wow, maybe since before hell. He thought through his own experiences with her and found that she'd even made him smile a few times. Maybe, *that's why she is here.* His lips even pulled back at the thought now. Could the Father have sent a peace offering? And to think, Ramatel had almost thrown it back in his face.

If the peace offering had been anyone other than the beautiful, stubborn, redhead waiting in his room, he would have. Part of him still wanted to, just to show the Father that he was still pissed off, but his conversation with Jahi rang in his head.

"I can't forgive him Jahi."

'I'm not asking you to. Asking the Father to be with Clara doesn't equal forgiveness, although it might be the very beginning of fixing a broken relationship."

Ramatel watched Clara leave the meeting, grateful that she hadn't stayed to talk with Gabriel. He headed for the kitchen to pack food for the stakeout. This time he even slipped some extra things into the bag for her, like the chocolate she reached for when she was in the pantry and thought no one was watching, and barbeque potato chips. She really liked those he'd noticed. He wished he could pack a bottle of wine and two glasses, but it probably wouldn't do to have a drunk stakeout partner.

Liwet came in holding the baby. They regarded each other, both expressionless. Liwet spoke first, although his voice sounded gravelly.

"Will you tell me what you learned about her?" He sounded pained.

"Yes, tomorrow I will tell you everything, but tonight I'm late."

Liwet nodded and turned to walk away, doing the bouncy baby step as he retreated. Ramatel watched him go. *Saying goodbye to that baby is going to kill him.*

As Ramatel made his way to the house, his thoughts returned to his own issues. *Yes,* he thought, *tonight he'd tell Clara everything too, and hope to God it wasn't too late to stop her from hating him.*

Speaking of late though, the decision making portion of the meeting had taken and long time, with a lot of ideas suggested and dissected. All in all, they'd decided they needed a lot more information to alert the lesser angels and to put all hands on deck in stopping Philotanus and any other demons in play. Ramatel checked his watch. They needed to get posted up ASAP.

Clara must have taken the fastest shower in history and changed because she was ready to go when he returned. Neither of them spoke though. He sensed she was still pissed off, but she was still here, and that was something. He approached her and held out his arm.

"Ready?"

"Ready."

In the blink of an eye they were on another dusty rooftop. Ramatel did a visual scan of the perimeter, then walked it to ensure there was no awaiting danger. Clara had settled down to watch the club, which was diagonal from where they were.

Ramatel watched her for a moment. The warm wind had picked up some of her hair and was tossing it around behind her. Her tight shirt made the roundness of her hips standout. She sat still and more upright than usual. She was tense, obviously still hurt.

He sat down beside her. She'd picked a good spot to watch from. She had learned a lot in the last few days. She knew to be downwind when possible, to hide in the shadows, to bring a sweatshirt, to keep a weapon handy. She could differentiate the normal club goer behavior from cronie behavior and recognize them almost at a glance. He was proud of her.

"You wanted to talk?" she asked through obviously clenched teeth.

He flinched at her tone and tried to think of where to begin. "I... ugh... yeah. Clara, I'm sorry about last night."

She shrugged nonchalantly. "There is nothing to be sorry for, you didn't do anything wrong. I obviously misread our relationship. It won't happen again. I'm still planning on talking to Gabriel."

"No, you didn't misread anything Clara."

"But it doesn't matter, does it?" she spat out. He opened his mouth to answer but she interrupted him. "Don't bother answering that, I saw the way you looked at me last night."

"How did I look at you last night?"

"Like you hated me. Like I disgusted you," she said barely above a whisper. Her shoulders sank down and she drew her knees up to hug them.

It wasn't you I was disgusted with. He moved to hug her, but caught a whiff of a familiar and revolting scent in the air.

Malphas.

His thoughts shot back to a dark time, when he'd been strung up in the pit awaiting the next round of torture. There was always a new contender, and after a new contender broke the angel of endurance in a record time they would sign their name. He reached for his forearm where he knew this scar would be. It was curved with the hard lines of squares drawn through it, the moniker of the demon he now smelled.

"What is it?" Clara asked.

"Stay here." Ramatel cloaked himself and peered over the rooftop to the sidewalk below. His nemesis was there, surrounded by a horde of lesser demons. They were in human form, but they reeked of evil.

Ramatel drew both of his blades from his belt, stood up, and sprouted his wings. With a leap from the building, he launched himself at the horde, loosening his hold on the invisibility cloak the moment he began to scatter demon pieces.

The lesser demons attempted to strike in pairs and trios, but Ramatel was too fast for them, his hatred burning in his blood. He wedged demons in between himself and others, using them as shields while their horde mates attacked their own trying to get to him. He sliced the hand off one and kicked another into the street. He severed the femoral artery causing one demon to fall and bleed out on the sidewalk. He slammed his knives into necks and ribs, splashing the wall of the building with black demon blood like it was some kind of modern art display.

When he'd finally removed the obstacles between him and Malphas, Ramatel closed the distance with a snarl on his face. Mercy would not be shown on this night. Ramatel caught the demon by the hair as it attempted to flee, and opened the skin on its bicep with his knife. His blade followed through slicing across its chest, not deep enough to hit bone, just enough to open the skin and muscle. Black slime spilled out the demon.

Ramatel turned his hand over when he'd run out of demon body to carve and began anew, carving in the opposite direction now. When he'd made two gashes across it's chest, he aimed for the belly, then sliced straight up stabbing into its chin. It was the sound of Clara's whimper that brought him out of his blood lust and made him finally drive a dagger through the demon's heart.

Ramatel glanced up to the roof expecting to see Clara's terrified face watching the whole scene but she wasn't there. *Oh God, has she run from me?*

***

At first, Clara had thought Ramatel was just finding some excuse to avoid talking until she saw his face. If she had thought there was hate on his face the night before she'd been wrong, because there was no mistaking that look now. His features had scrunched, and his eyes narrowed. They even darkened and he bared his teeth like a wolf. His entire body went rigid then disappeared from sight.

She crawled quietly to the edge to watch him destroy the demons below. Ramatel was both frightening and beautiful to watch. He swung his arms and legs with perfect precision, as if he knew where the demon's blows were going to be ahead of time. His knives sliced through flesh and punctured bones. He moved like some invisible force was keeping him just off the ground, and at a speed Clara could barely make her eyes keep up with. The demons never stood a chance.

A crunching sound on the dusty debris and the bird shit littering the roof brought her attention back to her own surroundings. She turned her head slowly and found herself facing the muzzle of a pistol.

Clara's eyes widened as the realization of the danger she was in hit her. She didn't recognize the demon holding the gun, but she also barely glimpsed in his direction. Her eyes were glued to the muzzle and she felt the familiar fear of her nightmares overtake her body.

She froze in sheer terror.

All of her training seemed to leave her, taking rational thought with it. She pictured the muzzle flash that had killed her. The bright light that ended all light. She knew it was going to come from this pistol before her. She wasn't sure how she knew, or if that was realistic, but she felt it in her body as sure as her next heartbeat. There would be about five more seconds and the flash would go off.

Five. *There is so much left to do!*

Four. *I haven't finished saving my soul!* Clara felt something warm on her leg as she counted down the seconds.

Three. *I've only had a few weeks with Ramatel!*

Two... *I am about to die!*

Blackness.

Chapter Sixteen

Clara awoke back in her bedroom in Ramatel's arms.He was carrying her to the bathroom. She lifted her head and looked down at her body. *Alive. I'm alive.*

"I'm alive?"

"Yes, Sweetie. You're alive."

She fidgeted and he put her down in the bathroom. "What happened?"

He gave her that placating smile. "Shh, you need to take a shower. I'll get your pajamas."

"Ok," she replied dumbly, her brain still seemed to be on the fritz.

Clara started to undress, pulling her shirt over her head. She wasn't sure what the change in Ramatel was tonight, but then again, thinking was hard right now. It felt like someone had put her brain on ice. She moved to pull her pants off and found them wet in the crotch. Then she remembered.

The gun. The muzzle.

She had wet herself.

Her first actual combat scenario with a demon and she had hidden on the roof and wet herself. Ramatel had been right. She couldn't handle this. She was mortified. Shame and humiliation heated her body. She was nothing more than a child playing at a grown-up role. She wanted to cry. She wanted to hit something. She wanted to go back and beat that demon to death. All that time she'd insisted on training, fighting... and she wet herself on the first go.

What would the others say? What did Ramatel think of her? Was an "I told you so," on the way? It ought to be. She deserved it.

She slumped her body onto the shower floor and reached for the nozzle. The spray was cold when it hit her. It felt appropriate though, like she deserved it. She shouldn't get hot water. Hot water was for big girls who didn't wet themselves. Clara hugged her knees and shivered under the water, eventually finding the strength to soap off and wash her hair.

Ramatel had left her pajamas and underwear as he'd promised, and she donned them. She really hoped he wasn't there when she stepped out of the bathroom. She wanted to go hide in a corner and never be found again. She wished she could just disappear and never face anyone again.

He was there when she opened the door. She stared at the floor, unable to meet his eye.

"How are you?"

I'm a coward. I didn't even fight back. I never should have been there in the first place. You were right. I should have listened to you. I'm stupid, so stupid, and incapable. "I'm okay," she squeaked out when she found her voice. She felt that her voice was higher than usual. *Just breath, Clara. Don't add to your shame by crying now.*

Ramatel approached her, blocking her way to her bed. "Honey..." he wrapped his arms around her. "-you're freezing. Did you use the hot water?"

She shrugged limply in his arms.

"Come here," he lifted her and carried her to his bed. He pulled the sheets back and draped her body on the bed.

She let him. She had no fight, no energy, no motivation left in her. It felt like she wasn't in her body at all. Her body had betrayed her anyway. She didn't want to come back to it.

Ramatel climbed in beside her and covered them both. He pulled her into his arms and held her tightly. She wanted to cry, but crying was a luxury she didn't deserve. She didn't deserve self-pity.

After some time, she felt herself drifting off to sleep, anxious for the reprieve from reality. She made about 5 minutes into dreamland when a gun went off in her face. She jolted into the air, landing again on the bed, stiff and as frightened as ever.

Ramatel tightened his grip and petted her hair. She forced herself to close her eyes again and tried to relax into him. Eventually her breath slowed and a gentle sleep began to pull at her. Within minutes she jumped again at the same image. This went on throughout the entire night until about five in the morning when her exhaustion got the better of her.

***

Ramatel lay there with Clara in his arms all night. Every time she jerked herself awake a piece of him broke. *I should have been there with her. I never should have left her alone. I was selfish. I went to go exact revenge and left her alone. She must hate me. She won't even look at me.*

He held her until the morning, when it seemed she had finally drifted off to sleep, then he decided he would have food waiting for her when she awoke, so he left to prepare some.

He also needed to tell Gabriel what had happened with the demons. *Would he be awake? Then again, does he ever sleep?*

Within the hour, Ramatel found himself in Gabriel's study.

"So Malphas made it topside?" Gabriel asked.

"Not anymore, I killed him." Ramatel said. "There's more. One of the lesser demons got to Clara. He pointed a gun at her and she fainted. She's been having nightmares all night."

Gabriel nodded. "Isn't that how she died the first time?"

Oh shit, it was. I let her relive her death! Ramatel put his head in his hands. No one else ever had to confront something that had literally killed them before. "I never should have left her alone. She wanted to leave me. She wanted you to ask the Father for a new *chinsen.* I should have let her."

Gabriel put his hand on Ramatel's shoulder. "It doesn't work that way, and I would have refused. You two were paired together for a reason."

"So she could nearly get killed?"

"But she did not, and you wouldn't have left her there if you thought that would happen. It is in the past now. What you need to worry about is damage control. Go help her heal from this."

Ramatel nodded. He picked up the grocery bag of breakfast food and headed back to his room.

Clara was awake when he got there. She was hugging her knees again, and back on her own bed. She still didn't meet his eyes. She looked like a shell of the woman he knew. There was no life in her eyes, no gleam, no defiance, just… a hollow emptiness. He offered her food but she said she wasn't hungry.

"Thank you, but I just want to be alone at the moment."

Ramatel obliged, leaving the food there in case she got hungry. He kept his distance all day, but remained nearby so he'd be able to return in an instant. First, he sat in the living room where he could see if the bedroom door opened, pretending to sharpen and clean his knives. Eventually he moved to the lawn watching the door to the back house like a puppy.

She hates me now.

Liwet found him sitting beside the pool trying to read up on Molech, except that he kept reading the same paragraph over and over. Liwet still cradled the sleeping baby in his arms. Ramatel was beginning to think he never put her down.

"Is this a good time?" Liwet asked.

Ramatel closed the book. "Good as any I guess."

"Where was she from? Does she have any family?"

"We were in a Mexican town called Nochixtlán. It looks like a nice town at first, but it's run by cronies. I don't know which house was hers specifically. All the families were slaughtered. The bodies had been moved by humans in most cases."

"Do you think she still has family?"

Ramatel shrugged. "Odds are likely, but trying to track them down is going to a bitch. It's doable. Probably. I think." He paused briefly. "I don't know actually. She's awfully young. Even if we go showing pictures to the neighbors and asking about family, with six kids missing, she might not get to the right house." Ramatel sighed. "Then again, if the family was close she might."

Liwet nodded, but Ramatel couldn't read his expression. He was staring at the baby who'd awoken and was playing with his finger. He stood to leave. "Thank you."

Chapter Seventeen

Clara hid in the room all day, grateful that Ramatel gave her space. He hadn't shown her anything but kindness. No self-righteous declarations of his prior statements about her not belonging in the fight. He didn't need to. It was as obvious as the dampness on her pants had been. Ramatel came to check on her and offer different food a few times, but she didn't eat. She wasn't hungry. What did she need the calories for? Obviously not for fighting. They would be better being used for someone who could contribute. Ramatel even offered her a drink once, but she couldn't accept it. She wasn't worthy of the escape the liquor offered, and certainly not of celebration.

Eventually, well into the evening, she fell asleep. Her sleep was again plagued by nightmares, but this time they'd morphed. The demon holding the gun rotated through her friends. They were laughing at her, holding her at gunpoint now on a stage where everyone laughed.

She felt Ramatel lift her and carry her to his bed. She opened her eyes to see him gazing down at her with a pained expression. They didn't speak, but she felt him wipe away tears that were running down her cheeks. Her cheeks burned with shame and she buried her head in his chest, unable to meet his eye anymore.

The next day brought more moping in the morning until Ramatel had said that most of them were going to look at the power plant. What Clara actually heard was "I'm going to leave you here, alone and unguarded."

Her eyes went wide with fear and she felt her bottom lip trembling. She didn't want him in the room to witness the evidence of humiliation, but at the idea of a separation she ran cold with panic. She pictured demons attacking her with pistols. Who would help her? Evidently she couldn't rely on her own skill.

"Baby, I'll stay if you need me too." She nodded furtively and he embraced her. "Okay..." he agreed, "but you gotta get out of this room honey. Do you want to come eat with the rest of us?"

He body tensed again. Looking the others in the eye sounded just as bad as facing that pistol again. He must have noticed the reaction. "You don't have to. What about a picnic, just us? Let you get some sunshine?"

"Yeah, okay"

"I know a secluded place in the valley..."

Outside the estate?! Where demons could reach her?! "No!"

"Okay, okay. In the garden then?"

She nodded.

Ramatel packed a lunch for them and took Clara by the hand to the door of the back house. When he stepped through the door she hesitated to follow. She had to look around to make sure no danger was waiting for her.

What if... She knew that it was crazy to think demons had managed to get on Gabriel's estate, through his wards and whatever else, and bypassed all the angels just to attack her, but she had to check. With the area visibly cleared, she allowed herself to follow Ramatel.

He already had a blanket spread out there, but she couldn't resist the compulsion to look behind her again, in case a demon had come since the last time she'd cleared her path of retreat. Then a glance in the other directions which yielded no threats, and a sweep of potential hiding spots in each direction reminded her how crazy she was being. She could feel Ramatel studying her, but she couldn't make herself stop this.

She managed to choke down part of the sandwich, but turned down the chocolate that he offered. *I don't deserve chocolate. Chocolate is for big girls who don't wet themselves.* He frowned her declination of chocolate, but didn't push.

"We're coming up with a plan of attack for the summer solstice," Ramatel informed her, trying to draw her into a conversation. "Gabriel is even bringing any local lesser angels who can fight. He was talking about having you and Jahi transport humans back here or to the cage."

The cage was a large warehouse that Gabriel owned. It literally had a cage for demons that they didn't want to kill yet.

Clara withdrew into herself and hugged her knees again. Ramatel moved behind her to massage her shoulders.

"I...I... I don't think I can do it Ramatel," she spoke softly.

"Do what? I thought you said you could drive?"

"I don't think I can fight anymore."

He stopped massaging and leaned around to look at her. He crooked his finger around her chin and brought her face to his. "I won't make you, but please just think about it?"

She nodded. She knew thinking wasn't going to help though.

***

Ramatel awoke alone late the next morning. Clara wasn't sleeping with him or in her bed. He supposed he should consider that a good sign. At least she was up and about today. He went to use the bathroom but sat back down when he noticed something. The laundry basket was missing from the room. The one that had been the point of contention. She was serious about not fighting anymore.

Somehow, up until now he hadn't wanted to believe his own eyes telling him that her spirit had broken, but seeing the laundry basket missing was undeniable.

He'd just managed to get pants on when he heard a knock at the door.

"Hey," Jahi greeted him when he answered the door. "Is Clara here?"

Ramatel opened the door wide and let her in. "No," he said sadly.

"Where is she?"

"I think she has decided to quit fighting and become house staff."

Jahi frowned. "What makes you think that?"

Ramatel pointed to the empty space where the laundry basket should be. "She took the laundry basket, the one that we fought about in the beginning."

"Is this about what happened the other night on the roof? Michael said she fainted." Jahi sat down on the folding chair, so Ramatel sat on the unmade bed.

"Yeah, she got a gun in her face, like the way she died before, and she fainted. Then yesterday she said didn't think she could fight anymore. She has nightmares all through the night now."

"Does she talk about it?"

Ramatel shook his head. "She barely talks at all. I think she's mad at me for leaving her alone on the roof."

"You were fighting a horde weren't you?"

Ramatel's head nodded, and he absent mindedly touched the scar on his forearm. "It was Malphas and his gang, but I shouldn't have left her alone. Now she barely even talks to me."

"If you had known she'd be in danger would you have left her alone?"

"Of course not!" he barked, as he stood and began to pace the room.

"You can't blame yourself for not acting on something you didn't know was going to happen."

"I should have known," he raked his hand through his hair.

Jahi shrugged. "You are the angel of foretelling are you?" Ramatel gave Jahi an irritated look, but she continued. "So chalk it up to lesson learned and go apologize to her."

"Aren't you listening? She hates me, she won't hear me." He turned and paced in the other direction.

"Have you tried?"

Ramatel sat back down and let his silence answer for him.

Jahi nodded. "I'm going to go talk to her, then I'm going to send her to talk to you." Then Jahi's voice rose an octave and she spoke patronizingly like she was talking to a toddler. "Use your words like a big boy."
Ramatel grabbed a boot from the floor to hurl at Jahi, but she was already out the door. The boot hit the wall near the door. "See? That's what I'm talking about," she called behind her. "Words!"

Chapter Eighteen

That morning Clara decided that Ramatel's attempts to get her out of the house were a sign that it was time to quit moping. She had already disappointed him once, and she wouldn't do it again. If being a *chinfon* meant servitude, then serve she would. Especially if it also meant she never had to leave the house again. She finished putting the laundry in the dryer and was about to return to mopping in the foyer.

"Hey," a voice behind her called. Clara jumped away from the voice bringing her mop up in a defensive hold.

"Whoa, it's just me," Jahi said putting her hands up in front of her.

Clara lowered the mop, but still looked past Jahi for any lingering threats that may have followed her in from the hall.

"You okay?" Jahi asked.

Clara pinched the bridge of her nose. "No, not really."

Jahi beckoned for Clara to follow her and they sat in the kitchen while Jahi made tea. "Well from what I heard happened, that's understandable."

"What did you hear?" Clara asked in a monotone.

"Someone put a gun to your face and you fainted." Jahi set two mugs out.

Clara nodded. "Did you hear what happened before that?"

"Ramatel went to fight an old enemy."

"They were enemies?"

Jahi nodded and poured hot water into the cups. She added tea bags. "I'll let him tell you about that."

"Did he tell you I wet myself?"

Jahi shook her head. "No, but isn't that a normal human reaction to that kind of fear, like a parasympathetic nervous system kind of thing?"

"I don't know." Clara tried to sip the tea but it was too hot. There was a moment of silence. "He was right Jahi. I'm not cut out for this. I had one actual combat meeting and I blew it. I put us both in danger because he had to come rescue me."

"I seem to recall another one where you kicked ass."

"That wasn't really a combat situation."

Jahi stirred some sugar into her tea. "Oh it was. I promise. You just preempted the strike."

Clara pinched her lips together in a "whatever" look. "I still put him in danger. What if I do that every time I face a gun? I'm useless as a fighter and the worst part is he knows it. He knows he was right and he's being extra nice to me now because he doesn't want to rub it in. This is actually worse."

Jahi rolled her eyes. "Yeah sure, that's the only reason he has for being nice to you."

"Well since I've become this subservient woman, he's been hugging me, planning picnics, and sleeping with me at night."

Jahi smirked and raised a questioning eyebrow.

Clara anticipated the question. "No. No sex."

Jahi sighed. "Look Clara, you had a normal reaction to something that literally killed you once. I think that with enough time and practice we can even get you used to

fighting guns. Michael has been known to work miracles."
She grinned.

Clara was silent and looking at the table. "I'm scared
Jahi," she whispered.

"That's why it's important to go slow. You want me
to talk to Michael?"

"I don't know." There was a moment of silence.
"You won't tell him about my accident will you?"

"Of course not, but just so you know, he wouldn't
care. None of us would. We've all been around long
enough to see and experience fear, but I think you should
talk to Ramatel."

Clara snorted. "Yeah, for all the good it's done me so
far."

Jahi smiled. "He might surprise you this time."

"Fine," Clara said, pushing her chair back. She
parted ways with Jahi and headed back to her house, only
to find an empty room. A note on the desk read "Had to go
check out the plant with Asael. Be back soon. -R"

***

Ramatel knew what he had to do. He'd been
pondering it all day when he should have been paying
attention at the power plant. While Asael had been busy
mapping out possible entry and exit points, attack
positions, and defensible positions, Ramatel had been lost
in his own thoughts.

He decided that he would go speak to the Father and
ask for permission to deepen his relationship with Clara,
but he would wait until after the solstice. With the amount
of hostility Ramatel was still harboring against the Father,

there was no telling if he would return from the trip or be cast back into hell, and his team of angels would need him. Tonight he would begin practicing what to say with Jahi.

Ramatel found Clara scrubbing the grout between tiles in the foyer when he returned to Gabriel's estate. His breath caught as he watched her curvy figure sway to the motion of the cleansing. He longed to cup those hips, then he cursed himself for thinking that when she was doing something he knew she hated.

"Clara," he started but stopped when she jumped at the sound of his voice. There was some kind of new expression on her face when she saw him.

Relief.

His chest swelled when he saw that she was happy to see him but deflated when he remembered why. He approached her and squatted to be at the same level as her. She was on her knees on the floor. He took the cleaning cloth from her hands and replaced it with his own hand.

"Can we talk?" he asked.

She nodded and left the cloth and bucket on the floor as she stood. Ramatel led her back to their room in silence. Once there, he sat her on his large bed and joined her.

She's still barely looking me in the eye. "You don't have to clean, you know?" he started. *Dammit, what was he saying? That came out wrong.*

"I thought you wanted me to clean," she replied weakly.

"I… I did. I don't anymore. Now I want you to fight. We *need* you there at the solstice."

She fidgeted with her hands but didn't look up. "No, you were right. I'm never going to be strong enough to take on a demon."

His heart broke at her words. He'd planted this idea in her head.

Ramatel got up from the bed and headed to his closet. He returned with a machete, a sword, a pistol, a small butterfly knife, and a pair of nunchucks and laid them all out on the floor in front of her. He crossed his arms and stood over the weapons. "Which one is the best weapon here?"

Clara eyed the display. "For what?"

"For everything."

She thought about the various differences between each. "That depends on what you want to do with it."

"Exactly Clara. You may not be strong enough to take on a demon in hand to hand combat, but that doesn't mean you're useless." He picked up the butterfly knife. "I wouldn't try to behead someone with this, but it would work better in an up-close fight than that pistol. This is you Clara. Small but effective. You still have a place with us."

She reached for the knife and brought it back to her lap. Her fingers curled around the hilt. She absentmindedly tested the sharpness of the blade gently against her thumb. She continued to study it long enough for him to decide that she wasn't convinced.

"Clara, I... I'm sorry. I shouldn't have left you alone."

Clara burst into tears so suddenly that it startled Ramatel. He sat down and put his arms around her.

"I put you in danger because I freaked out at the gun. You had to come rescue me." Her chest bounced with sobs. She took another deep breath. "I thought you wanted me to clean. You were being so nice to me." Sob.

"Ramatel I can't do it. I can't go back into the field. I'm a liability."

"Sshhh. You were never a liability. We should have anticipated this as soon as you told us how you died. I'm as much to blame as that demon."

She pulled away and shook her violently. "No."

"C'mere." He tugged her back into his embrace. "I only wanted you to clean because I was an idiot. I know you weren't cut out to be a maid. I saw how much you loved fighting with Michael. You even made Asael smile. I don't think I've seen him smile in two thousand years. Clara this is what you were born for. You can't tell me you're happy scrubbing floors?"

There was no comment, but after a moment she shook her head. "Aren't I supposed to be here to serve though?"

"You are here to right some kind of wrong from a past life. Not to be punished. If you hate cleaning that would be punishment, and if God wanted to punish you, he would have sent you into the abyss. Clara you were sent to be a fighter."

"I just don't know if I can do it anymore."

"We need you to do it Clara." That wasn't entirely true. They could use a lesser angel to get the humans away from the power plant, but he was hoping this would motivate her to try again. Ramatel would have preferred that Clara be safely tucked away at Gabriel's, but he also knew that if she cleaned for the rest of her life she would never fix the part of her that was broken. She needed to confront this fear.

"Command me to do it."

"Clara I won't ever command you to do anything ever again."

"No, I need you to. I don't think I can do it if you don't command me."

Ramatel looked into those brilliant green eyes. The whites were red from crying still. "Fine. Clara, fight with us on the solstice," he commanded.

Clara waited for her body to feel compelled to do something. "Did you do it? That felt different."

"Last time the command took effect immediately. This was for a future time. You'll feel it when it takes effect.

Clara nodded. "Thank you."

There was another silence while Ramatel thought about what to say next. "Clara I want to ask the Father if we can be more than *chins*."

She drew back and stared into his face. "You're not… ashamed of me?"

This baffled Ramatel like she'd just thrown ice water on him. "Why would I be ashamed of you?"

"I wet myself."

"What?" He tried to stifle a laugh. "You think I'm ashamed because of that? Honey, I spent two thousand years in hell. I've seen millennia old demons wet themselves. No, I'm not ashamed of you." She was still giving him that incredulous look. "I can't be certain how it's going to turn out though. It's hard to have faith in God's mercy when you've been on the receiving end of his vengeance. I have to wait until after the solstice, just in case he picks vengeance. These guys," he tipped his head toward the main house, "are going to need me at the fight."

"You think He would hurt you just for asking?"

"I don't know. Probably, not for asking. It's just that I have a lot of anger directed His way. I need to keep my cool so I don't piss Him off."

"Can you do that?"

"Jahi is helping me."

"By pissing you off?" They laughed together.

"I think He will say 'yes,'" Clara decided. She leaned into him and put her head on his chest.

Ramatel pinched his lips together wishing he had her faith. But, damn, with his relationship with the Father, the Father might punish him just for thinking it. Then again, if he slept with Clara without asking he would definitely be punished, and if he didn't ask, there was no chance.

Chapter Nineteen

Clara spent the next two days working with Michael and Ramatel on weapons training. Michael had started by merely pointing a finger at her, then a plain stick, then a knife, then a wooden gun. Finally, at the end of the second day, Michael brought out a real pistol. He showed it to her and let her see that it wasn't loaded.

"I'm going to point this at you, the same way I did with the wooden knife. Just do the exact same thing you did with the training gun."

Clara's stomach knotted. *Can I do this?* Images of the muzzle flash disrupted her thoughts. Her body tensed.

"You can do this Clara," Ramatel said from the edge of the mat. "Take a deep breath. It's just like the wooden one and you know it's not loaded."

Clara nodded, but she wasn't confident. She turned to Michael. He made eye contact and raised the pistol to Clara's face. She instantly turned her body sideways and used her forearm to push Michael's arm so the gun was no longer pointed at her. Her arm snaked over his bicep then under his forearm and she leaned her weight over the arm, causing him to go down in order to avoid a broken elbow. Actually, he was mimicking what the normal reaction would be. In reality, he probably could have just snatched his arm back, but using angelic strength wasn't going to help Clara.

Ramatel cheered from the sidelines. "You did it!"

Clara saw a big grin on his face and couldn't help but smile back. She wanted to go over and kiss that grin, but she knew she had to wait until they had permission from the Father.

The training continued over and over with Michael. They practiced with different pistols, different angles, and different techniques. Finally, after many hours, Michael called Clara over.

He pulled the bolt back of the 9mm they just been using. The brass metal casing of a bullet in the chamber glimmered in the light. It had been loaded! She wasn't sure if she should hit him or hug him.

"You did it Clara. I think you are ready."

She looked at Ramatel for reassurance. "You are ready Clara," his deep voice declared.

***

Gabriel summoned each of the key players to a meeting two days before the solstice. He'd asked for help from other angels and tonight they would be going over their plans. The meeting was scheduled for 5 pm, to be followed immediately by an informal dinner. Clara and Ramatel left their room together and joined Asael and Barakel in the living room of the back house before heading over.

"You ready for the first round of the battle?" Asael asked Ramatel in greeting.

Ramatel frowned. "Let's get this shit over with."

"What's do you mean?" Clara asked Asael.

There is something different about him today...
Asael looked stunning and menacing, more so than usual, and Clara tried to narrow down what had changed.

"You'll see," he replied and his long legs carried him out the door with Ramatel, Clara, and Barakel following behind.

Clara was anxious to meet the other angels. She'd only seen those she lived with on the estate. She wondered if there would be other *chinfons* here too.

Asael stopped just outside the door to the grand dining room and locked eyes with Barakel who remained as stoic as ever. When Barakel nodded slightly, Asael pinched his lips together and opened the door.

Clara couldn't see into the room yet, but she heard the chatter of conversation come to an abrupt stop when Asael and Barakel walked in. Ramatel placed a hand on her lower back appearing to usher her toward the door, but Clara sensed apprehension in his touch. A longing to hold his hand swept down her arm, but she wasn't sure how much affection was appropriate to display in front of other angels, so she let herself be guided into the room.

About twenty unreadable but beautiful faces stared at her. The men and women came in all shapes and sizes and appeared to be like humans, but humans who were at their peak physical potential. There were no errant hairs, no stray marks, no extra pounds, and no crows feet. Under their scrutiny Clara became hyper aware of every flaw, every scar, every dark spot on her body.

Most were generally smaller than the angels she lived with, but a couple of the males were still large. The khakis, business suits, and celestial white robes contrasted sharply with the black utility pants, stained t-shirts, and dangerous weapons worn by her crowd. There were two women in the corner wearing the scrubs of medical professionals, who still managed to pull those off like runway models.

The golden eyes of the crowd were wandering across the scarred, pierced, and bearded faces of the newly arrived, but those eyes took flight whenever eye contact was made. No warm smiles greeted them, not even a head tip of acknowledgement. A hushed whisper began to creep over the silence. The whisperers always turned away from the newly arrived to direct their voices elsewhere. The table remained open and empty as the other angels were all meandering around in small groups so the three fallen and Clara took up seats, and the whispering began to climb to a dull drone of conversations around them.

"Friendly lot," Clara whispered to Ramatel. He only nodded, but scrubbed a hand over the scar on his face.

"We're like convicted felons sitting at an aristocratic dinner party," Asael explained.

Clara studied the crowd as they studied her. "Are there any other *chinfons?*"

"No, it's highly unusual to bring a *chinfon* to a battle discussion, let alone a battle," Ramatel explained. Ramatel and Barakel sat slightly hunched over the table, both propping their heads up with their arms. Occasionally, Ramatel would find excuses to touch Clara, an arm pat, a slight shoulder rub. But he never let his touch linger. She wasn't sure if he was looking for reassurance from her presence, trying to lighten her apprehension, or trying to demonstrate his stake to the other angels in the room. She didn't mind, regardless of his reasons.

Asael sat upright and made a point to stare back at the golden eyes watching him with his own dark eyes, giving Clara a chance to examine him now. *Is that... eyeliner?*

Asael had a line of black kohl around his dark eyes, and black mascara appeared to lengthen his already full eyelashes. He had upgraded his fang piercings to a brighter pair than usual. Clara watched him flick those fangs at the faces of men who dared to look in his direction, and caught him winking at the pair of scrubs in the corner. The fair-haired one immediately blushed and turned away. The dark haired one made no sign that she had seen his wink, so he added a lewd gesture with his pierced tongue until she too looked away.

"What are you doing?" Clara asked him.

Asael barked a laugh in return. "Offending." He shot Clara a proud grin.

Clara was about to ask why when Jahi walked in with Butator, Liwet, and Hamal. The conversation again came to an abrupt halt.

"If you thought we were unwelcomed, imagine what they think of a demon whore," Asael whispered to Clara.

A wave of protectiveness for Jahi washed over Clara and she emphatically waved Jahi over with a smile, then got up to hug her when Jahi reached them. Jahi sat with Clara and the "kids" joined them. After a little while some of the newcomers began to approach the table, speaking first to Liwet and Hamal or trying unsuccessfully to engage Butator, who had started to rock slightly in his chair and stared at the table. The angels introduced themselves by name, some added titles after their names like "Zachriel, angel of memory," and "Andas, angel of air."

Clara leaned to Ramatel's ear. "What are you the angel of?"

He turned his head to whisper into her ear. "Inner strength…" he gave her earlobe a quick flick of his tongue that sent a wave of heat through her body, "and endurance." A teasing smile crossed his face as he pulled away from her.

"And the others?"

With a head tilt toward Barakel, Ramatel whispered "Lightning," then tilting his head toward Asael he whispered "Either punishment or metal work."

"Which is it?"

"I'm not sure." Ramatel replied, and Asael, who must have heard the conversation looked over at her and gave her a wink.

Clara's next question was interrupted when Gabriel and Michael walked in. Immediately, the atmosphere in the room changed. They were greeted like celebrities as the other angels gathered around them with smiles, handshakes, hugs, and questions about their wellbeing.

One of the larger of the angels, Zachriel, approached Michael and was received with an emphatic bear hug.

"Good to see you man! How've you been?" Michael exclaimed with an emphatic grin, not giving the man a chance to answer. "Are you back from New York now? Come meet my wife!" Michael strode up to Jahi and pressed a kiss to her lips, making the hall fall silent again, but only until Gabriel dropped a map on the center of the table.

"Okay, this is what we know…" he began, and launched an explanation of why they presumed Molech was up to something. He described the power plant, the solstice, the babies, Philotanus, and Xaphan. Then the discussion moved into the plan for tomorrow night's attack.

Clara listened to the battle plans and envisioned the upcoming fight. She was scared, she could admit that.

Terrified actually. *Is it too late to back out?* There would be demons trying to kill them there, with a hundred percent certainty.

She'd reached for Ramatel's hand under the table when her role was explained, and he gently squeezed it. A reassuring look from him told her of his faith. *I can do this. I have to. He commanded me.*

Clara and Jahi would be driving a van to transport human victims. Once they arrived at the plant, Jahi would lure the security guards away and Zachriel would put them into a fugue state, and replace the gate guard with his own *chinfon.* Barakel would be at the highest point, preferably on top of a smoke stack. Gabriel would be cloaked and waiting. He'd give the command to all the other fighters who would be waiting here at the estate. Babies were the first priority and should be flashed back here at all costs. Humans were next, and the plant was last. The two angels in scrubs were healers and they would be at Gabriel's estate on standby.

Gabriel and Michael fielded questions for about 45 minutes, which continued through dinner. The nerves in her stomach prevented Clara from eating so she pushed her food around her plate. As soon as dinner was officially over, she left immediately with all of the fallen and Jahi.

Chapter Twenty

Ramatel could tell from her pacing that Clara was nervous the day of the solstice. The lack of appetite, the clinging, and the extra energy gave it away. In their back house, they'd all gone over the plan again, the what-ifs, the backs up plans; somehow, everyone had ended up in their small living room. Even the kids, Gabriel, Michael, and Jahi were there. Ramatel suspected they'd come to ease their own nerves under the guise of checking on Clara.

Barakel was consistently charging himself up by fingering an electrical outlet. That was a much faster way than eating. Asael was sharpening daggers for everyone.

"Why don't we use guns more often?" Clara asked.

"It's takes a heavenly infused metal to kill demons. The powder burn that launches the bullet out of guns diminishes the infusion, so it isn't reliable," Michael explained.

"Fortunately, it works both ways," Gabriel added.

Asael disappeared into his room and returned with a wide silver choker that glistened in the light. "Since we're all here…" he cast a look around the room, "try this on." He handed the choker to Clara.

It had very intricate engravings on it that resembled the demon ward she'd learned, but these were slightly different markings. The lines were in different places and it held squiggly designs that she presumed were letters that she couldn't read. The intricacy of the artwork was astonishing. He must have spent months working on this.

Clara reached out for the choker and held it carefully as though she was afraid to break it.

"It's to protect you from the sexual demons, like Philotanus. Just in case he is there" Asael explained. "Let's try it out."

Ramatel couldn't help the wave of jealousy as he saw the look of appreciation and wonder on Clara's face. It should have been him to give her jewelry, even if Asael was the only one who could ever hope to make anything like that.

Ramatel stepped forward, damned if Asael was going to put it on her too, and he took the choker from Clara's hand. She turned around and lifted her hair while he clasped the metal behind her neck. She fingered the necklace and gave Asael an adoring look that made Ramatel want to hit him, even if Asael was only doing it to protect her and ensure the success of the mission.

Jahi moved in front of Clara and all of the angels stepped away. "Let me know what you feel about me, even if you think it's embarrassing. Especially if it's lust."

Clara nodded and they all waited.

"Well?" Jahi asked after a moment of silence.

"Um, nothing. Am I supposed to feel something?"

Asael grinned. "As much as I would love to see that…" Michael and Ramatel glared at him, "no, lust means it's working."

"Ahem," Ramatel cleared his throat. "I got you something too." Not to be out done, Ramatel retreated to their room, and produced the bullet proof vest he'd gotten her the day before.

The beaming smile she gave him at the sight of it was enough to make him feel like his bones had gone soft. She tried it on and it fit perfectly. He helped her adjust it so the plates fit over her heart and lungs.

"Sorry it's so heavy. It's the lightest one I could find."

"No, it's not bad actually." She swung her arms up and around, ensuring she still had all the range of mobility she'd need.

The conversation turned to the vest with the other angels asking Ramatel about the ballistic plates, what caliber it would stop, the weight, etc. Asael returned to his sharpening, handing the angels back their blades and reaching for new ones. Ramatel and Clara snuck back to their room for the remaining hour before the other angels began to turn up.

Ramatel watched her pull the vest off over her head, forcing her shirt to tighten around her breasts as she reached up. He moved to her side to assist with the vest, and casually stroked her back when the vest was off.

She turned to face him and tugged him into an embrace. He loved the feel of her arms encircling him, but not the fear that he knew was driving it. Pulling her to the edge of the bed, he sat her on his lap, and tried to ignore the stirring in his crotch.

"I'm scared," she whispered in his ear.

"Me too, but fighting is your calling."

She nodded. There was a long moment of silence while they held each other. She nuzzled her little face into his neck and he held her tighter. Her nuzzles soon turned into kisses that heated his blood and he had to stop her.

"Not yet, honey. Soon. If we do it without permission, we will both be punished and I won't have you risk it."

"At least we'd be together. I'd go to hell for you," she whispered.

He pulled away to stare into her eyes. She was serious. God, how he loved this woman. "Let's hope it doesn't come to that. I promise I'll ask permission as soon as this is over tonight."

She smiled at him. "Okay, I'll wait."

They sat there holding each other, wondering what the night would bring, until a knock on the door told them it was time to head to the main house and begin the night.

Chapter Twenty One

When everyone had arrived, Clara saw that Maria had put out a spread of food, although few were eating it. The two medics had an ambulance and already had medical supplies and gurneys set out and waiting for use. They weren't a comforting sight. The angels, who were so eloquently dressed last night, now looked like someone's private military, though none of them came close to looking as intimidating as those from her own house. Clara spotted the other *chinfon,* already dressed as the security guard he would be replacing.

The hall was livid with nervous energy. Some people became loud and cheerful as if attempting to defy their nerves to alter their mood. Some were somber and seemed deep in thought or prayer. Clara had no idea how she was supposed to act. *Is there a pre-battle normal?* She latched onto Ramatel's hand and gripped it as if her life depended on it. A look around at her companions reminded Clara that they went into battle every night. They were far less tense than those around them.

The clock ticked the seconds away, and for Clara they seemed to both hurry and drag at the same time. Finally, Gabriel walked to the center of the room. "It's time."

He gave Jahi and Clara an expectant look and they both headed to the door toward the van parked in the driveway. Michael and Ramatel followed, as did Zachriel and his *chinfon,* both of whom would be riding with them. Michael embraced Jahi at the same time that Ramatel wrapped Clara in his arms.

"You don't take any unnecessary risks, okay?" he whispered. "You just get the humans, don't try to tangle with any demons, and don't go after any humans until one of us has cleared the path of demons, okay?"

Clara just nodded. "Please be careful," she whispered back.

"I will. I promise. Are you going to be alright with guns if there are any?"

"Thanks to you I will."

He pulled back and smiled. "Okay, I'll see you there very soon." Clara climbed into the passenger's seat and saw Ramatel grab Zachriel's arm and whisper something to him. Zachriel nodded, then he and his *chinfon* climbed into the van.

The drive took almost two hours with the Los Angeles traffic and the four of them tried to make polite conversation. The other *chinfon's* name was Alex. He'd been back on earth about three years, and helped out with a couple other battles. He mentioned that he was surprised to see a female *chinfon* in a battle, and earned himself a glare for it from Clara.

It was still plenty light out when they arrived. Jahi parked the van while Clara slid to the driver's seat. Everyone else got out. With a wave of his hand, Zachriel managed to turn the security guard manning the gate into a mindless body. The guard still understood English but seemed to forget everything else. Jahi lured him out of the security booth to a predesignated spot in the bushes, where he was bound and gagged, and would remain that way until the next morning.

Alex took over manning the gate and let Clara drive through to where she would wait just inside. Jahi and

Zachriel went in on foot to clear the plant humans in the same manner they'd used for the guard. Zachriel wiping their minds and Jahi luring them to the bushes where they were to remain.

"Ready?" Gabriel asked as his body corporealized in the passenger seat.

Clara jumped at the sudden intrusion. "Shit! What the hell Gabriel!"

"Sorry. I figured I'd wait here a while. How about pulling the van over there?" He pointed ahead. "Molech's idol is at that last stack."

Clara pulled behind some kind of large industrial looking building where they waited in silence. Gabriel kept flashing in and out as he checked on things in the plant. Clara was antsy and wished Jahi and Zachriel would hurry because it was starting to get dark.

The minutes dragged on. Hours passed. Still no word, but, then again, no news was good news. Finally, a sigh of relief escaped Clara's chest at the sight of Jahi. They'd returned and proclaimed the plant clear.

***

Ramatel waited with his little band of fallen angels, joined by Michael. There were few words between them, but he knew Michael was suffering with the same concern for the woman he loved being out in the world, waiting for danger. The whole of the angelic horde seemed quieter now that the sun was setting.

Well into the night, Gabriel's form materialized in the center of the room, narrowly missing the table's edge.

"It's time. So far we have eight babies and about ten women. Nineteen demons and counting."

With that command, angels began disappearing from sight, Ramatel included. They re-formed under a stairwell overlooking the canal that ran alongside the plant, all cloaked in invisibility, but they could see each other. Gabriel pointed to various positions and the angels took up guard. With a flap of his wings, Barakel pushed off the ground and headed for the neighboring cooling tower. Ramatel headed in the direction that Gabriel indicated and took cover behind an outbuilding of some sort. He was joined by Michael because they could see the van from that vantage point.

They could also see the demons in human form, many carrying bound women who seemed to be fighting their binds. Unfortunately, the women were fighting them out of desperation for lust. The writing bodies of the women were grinding themselves into the demons, trying to kiss or lick any part of skin they could reach. *Philotanus has already gotten to them.* Ramatel scanned for the demon, determined to deal out a punishment for what he'd done to Clara, but he wasn't there. Still, the sight of any demon this close to Clara made Ramatel uneasy.

In front of the women at the base of the tower, a colorful playpen of sleeping babies stood out against the gray tones of the plant.

Drugged?

"We should do it now before they get—" Michael's words were cut off by a roaring noise coming from the tower. Seven holes had been cut through the tower and steam erupted from them. Heat warmed his face and Ramatel looked up to see that an image of a bull now decorated the tower. Xaphan stood above the demons holding a heavy, leather-bound tome in his hand.

A flash of white light next to him told Ramatel that Michael had lit his sword. Another light on the far side said Gabriel had done the same thing. With that unspoken command, Ramatel dashed from his hiding spot, catching glimpses of the other angels all sprinting toward the demons. Above him, a flash of lightning flew from Barakel's palm, knocking Xaphan from the stairs he stood on.

One demon, who'd been wrestling with a woman, shifted into a man with the head of a bull, eliciting a scream from the woman who only seconds before had had her tongue in the demon's ear.

Morax, Ramatel thought, *the original minotaur. Figures he'd be here.* Ramatel shifted directions, and sprouted his wings.

The demon leapt back and released a bellowing roar. Its hand raised over its head and an incantation somehow flew from its inhuman mouth, accompanied by no small amount of spittle.

As Ramatel beat his wings, flying toward the bull-headed chanting man, he felt a strong weight plow into him from the side and his rush was abruptly halted. Ramatel looked down and saw that another horn-headed minotaur had hit him.

"He's summoning his legions!" one of the young angels cried.

Ramatel was pinned against a wall by the hand of a beast whose breath was heavy and hot on his face. A shiver of a memory from hell, when he was similarly

pinned, rose to his forethought and rage overtook
Ramatel's body.

    This time he was not bound and helpless.

    And he never would be again.

    He launched into a series of strikes against the beast
with a knife in each hand, stabbing and slicing through
skin and flesh. Within seconds he managed to gut the thing
and drive a blade deep into its neck. It fell hard, giving
Ramatel just enough time to free himself of its grasp
before catching another monster with his blades.

Chapter Twenty Two

Clara felt her mouth fall open at the sudden appearance of hundreds of minotaurs.

"Are you seeing this?" Jahi asked incredulously from Clara's side, her eyes large with shock as she stared out of the windshield.

"Uh huh," Clara uttered but her eyes remained fixed on the scene ahead of her.

Angels were engaged in hand to hand fighting with demons and bull-headed creatures everywhere. The monsters were at least seven feet tall and held none of the docility Clara was used to seeing in cattle. Steam poured from their nostrils mixed with something wet dripping from their noses. Their humanlike bodies resembled that of a man's but much larger and with cloven hooves rather than feet. Only a loin cloth covered their hairy skin.

Michael and Gabriel were creating a path through the minotaurs with their flaming swords, trying to allow others a chance to get to the babies, all of whom were screaming from the heat of the steam coming from the holes in the tower. Awash in glory, Michael was making quick lunges and dashes as he struck down the beasts in his path, who bellowed in pain when the blazing sword pierced their skin.

What Gabriel lacked in technique, he made up for in speed. It was hard to keep up with his movements as his sword gutted and sliced. Sweat was beginning to drip from his forehead, but he showed no sign of slowing.

Above them, Barakel was atop a building now, launching bolts of lightning at anything with horns that went near the babies. Thunder claps from each lightning strike filled the air and mixed with the occasional gunshot coming from the few demons still in human form. Smoke from the bodies of the monsters that were hit was beginning to fill the air, leaving a stench of burning hair and charred meat. Clara watched as another bolt struck a bull-headed monster in the back, and it fell with a cry of agony.

Ramatel was following the path toward the group of women and babies that Michael and Gabriel were clearing, while holding the demons at bay to let some of the lesser angels advance. One at a time, monsters fell to his knives, leaving a trail of horned bodies and black blood in his wake. Ramatel sliced, kicked, and stabbed his way up to Gabriel and Michael, then took a turn leading the pack through the monsters. Gabriel and Michael fell back to assist the newer angels, but Ramatel fought tirelessly, still barely even breathing hard.

One of the angels, *Andas,* Clara thought his name was*,* began redirecting the steam away from the babies with a stream of air blown from his lips. Liwet and Asael had peeled off from the pack and were approaching the babies from the back of the tower now. They each held only one knife in their right hands, leaving their less dominant hands open to make a quick snatch when they closed in on the playpen. Liwet's eyes were fixed on the babies and he wore a determined expression. Asael appeared to have a permanent snarl on his lips reminding everyone that he was still the most fearsome thing in this battle.

Zachriel who had flashed away to get Alex, temporarily leaving Clara and Jahi alone, returned to stand next to Jahi's window. Alex seemed none the worse for wear.

"Oh fuck!" Zachriel exclaimed when he saw the apocalyptic scene before them.

Michael and Gabriel were closing in on the women when Jahi yelled "Clara stay here. Zachriel let's go get the women."

Clara considered arguing for about a nanosecond, but she knew this battle was way beyond anything she could contribute to. Jahi and Zachriel disappeared, only to reappear in the midst of the gaggle of bound women, while the angels in the battle held the monsters at bay. Jahi and Zachriel began slicing at binds, only to be accosted by the lust driven humans, who groped and grabbed at their rescuers. Zachriel snatched the only two they'd managed to free and flashed them to the outside of the van.

"Leave them bound. Just get them here!" Clara cried, leaping from the van, just as Zachriel vanished again. One of the women was already trying to run after the demon horde again. Clara tackled her to the ground and wrestled an arm behind her.

"Get up," she ordered, trying to drag the sex deranged woman to her feet. The woman continued to struggle, making Clara tug the woman to her feet by her hair. She violently led the screaming woman back to van and pushed her into the side door, just in time to catch the next escapee by the wrists.

Zachriel returned with two more women, blessedly still bound this time. Jahi reappeared with him and tossed Alex a bag of zipcuffs that she must have found in the gaggle of women.

"Over here ladies," Jahi called teasingly as she climbed into the van. The women all chased after Jahi, stumbling over themselves to follow her into the van.

Alex and Clara followed, as Jahi lured them like the pied piper. Together they cuffed the women to anything in the van that wouldn't move, and re-emerged just in time for the next two women Zachriel brought. He tossed them into the back of the van and disappeared again. They did this twice more, until they'd secured all the women.

"Let's go!" Jahi yelled, climbing into the driver's seat. Alex and Zachriel clamored in over a pile of writhing women while Clara took the passenger seat.

Clara looked up to see Ramatel, Michael, Gabriel, and two other angels, holding a line of demons back while Asael snatched two babies and disappeared, leaving Liwet to defend the remainders until he could return. He would be taking them straight to Gabriel's dining room. Clara smiled seeing that Ramatel didn't even look winded.

A fiery figure appeared behind the remaining two babies. It was the demon that had once held the book, but now it looked as if the body and features were made of flame and cinder.

"No!" Clara screamed against the window as the van launched forward under Jahi's insistent and frightening driving.

"They'll save 'em, Clara!" Jahi yelled at her as they pulled away with screeching tires. Shots rang out as they sped off. The passenger window shattered and for some reason Clara felt something tickling her neck. She reached up to find herself bleeding.

"Oh," she managed as she leaned forward, feeling very dizzy suddenly.

"NOOOO!" she heard Jahi scream, but she sounded far away.

Chapter Twenty Three

Sending bolts in quick succession, Barakel hit the fiery figure with everything he had but the lightning didn't have any effect on Xaphan. If anything, it was just heating him even more. The fire demon advanced on the babies and Liwet, just as Asael returned for the remaining two infants. Asael dove in front of the babies, using his body to shield them from the scalding heat of Xaphan, while Liwet snatched the babies from the playpen that had collapsed at some point in the midst of all the chaos. Asael needed to give Liwet time to distance the babies from danger so he lunged at the fiery beast and released a scream of pain when his skin burned and bubbled under Xaphan's grasp.

Within what felt like eternal seconds, a tornado of water trailing all the way back to the canal slammed into both Xaphan and Asael, knocking them to the ground and extinguishing the fiery furnace of a demon just enough to allow Asael to plunge his blades into the being. The demon screamed, releasing a hiss of steam into the air before it died.

Ramatel looked around to see Hamal with his hands raised, controlling the wet funnel. Asael rolled his body off the demon and collapsed in the puddles on the ground. The water tornado moved into the mass of horned monsters and several were pulled upward by the force. The tornado carried them back to the canal, spinning up more monsters into the dizzying current. With the momentum of the battle now against them, the minotaurs ceased their advance and began to vanish, back to where they came from, while the angels sliced down any minotaurs that were too slow to escape their blades.

"Asael! Asael, you okay?!" Michael picked the bleeding angel off the ground. Some of his skin remained on the sopping wet pavement.

"I nng Okay," Asael tried to say back, but his lips had burned off. The skin around his face and torso had melted into piles in the pavement.

"Let's get you to the healers," Michael replied, trying to encircle the large man in his arms before they disappeared together.

As the battle died down and the clean-up began, Zachriel appeared on the concrete under the tower. "Ramatel," Zachriel called in a loud but somber voice.

Ramatel looked up from the injured minotaur he'd been finishing off.

"Come home. Now," Zachriel called insistently then vanished.

Ramatel gave Gabriel a confused look. Gabriel only nodded back as if giving permission to leave.

Ramatel re-formed in the dining hall that had turned baby nursery and medical aid station for the night. The babies seemed to be temporarily unattended, left in one of Sarah's blanketed pens. The beeps, cyclic air, and small engines of medical machines filled the air, mixed with the sound of wails from the babies. He turned his head to the right, seeing Asael being worked on by one of the healers. A glow radiated from her hands, shining light over Asael's chest.

Michael was in the far corner with another healer. Dark, red hair pooled on the ground from behind the cover of the healer's knee.

Red hair.

"Clara!" Ramatel flashed to the side of the healer, who was backing away. Clara lay in a pool of blood with a bandage pushed to her neck and towel underneath her. Her skin was paler than usual, making the freckles stand out even more.

"Clara!" Ramatel called, putting his hand on her shoulder to wake her. She didn't stir. She needed help. *Why aren't they helping her?!*

He grasped the healers shoulders. "Help her!" he commanded.

The healer shook her head. "I can't."

"Help her! She is hurt!" he shouted at the frightened woman.

The healer was trying to back away still. "I... I... can't. The artery was severed..."

Ramatel looked to Michael for help with this crazy healer and saw only a bereft expression.

"She is dead," the woman finally stated.

"NO!" Ramatel cried. "No! You fix her! Fix her now!" He shook the healer for everything she was worth. Michael intervened, pulling the healer from his arms and she fled.

"Ramatel," Michael started gently. "Clara's soul has left her body."

"NO!" Ramatel cried turning back to Clara. If they wouldn't help her, he would. He picked up the bandage and held steady pressure to her neck. Already he could see the bleeding had slowed.

"Clara. Clara answer me." Clara didn't move. There was no flutter to her eye lids, no pulse behind his bandage, no rise and fall of her chest.

"Clara please…" Ramatel begged, as the situation began to solidify in his mind. "Please Baby, come back."

The room behind him began to fill with angels returning. They began to whisper, asking "What happened?" about Clara, and "How is he?" about Asael.

"She is gone Ramatel," Michael said somberly behind him. "Feel for her soul. It has left."

Ramatel couldn't feel her soul anymore. Logically, he knew Michael was right, but he couldn't believe that. He wouldn't believe that. He pushed the bandage against her neck trying to protect the body that he had always known as Clara. Even without a soul it was his link to her. He felt he should protect it now, as he had failed to protect her.

Failed.

He'd failed to protect her. She didn't want to go into that battle. He had even tricked her into doing it. He had never used his *chinshen* commands on her.

"Clara. Oh, Clara I'm sorry. Clara please! Please come back," he begged. Ramatel ignored the sniffles and some quiet, jerking breaths of people crying behind him. With her body cradled in his arms, Ramatel clung to the only remaining connection to her that he had.

Someone approached him from behind. He felt Jahi kneel next to him. She must have returned from dropping off the women at the cage. He allowed her to linger with him because she loved Clara too, and a part of him was still cinched to the hope that maybe Clara would open her eyes. Maybe she would do it for Jahi. Maybe this was a bad dream and he would wake up.

Jahi reached out to take Clara's hand and wiped at her own tear filled eyes with her free hand. Long minutes of sobbing passed between them. Disappointment hit Ramatel again when Clara's eyes remained shut. Clara wouldn't open her eyes for Jahi either.

"I... I..." he tried to form words to Jahi. "I shouldn't have made her go. I should have protected her."

Jahi embraced him hard and squeezed his shoulders. "You needed to do that Ramatel. She needed you to push her, like you needed her to push you." They wept together at length, and later, finally spent, they pulled away from each other and Michael drew Jahi away.

Ramatel stayed with Clara throughout what was left of the night and into the morning. The lesser angels began saying their goodbyes and trickling out. The huffs and moans of Asael coming around broke the silence after an hour or so. He made some sort of inappropriate comment to the healer attending him and started asking questions about the others. He heard Michael tell him that Clara didn't make it and Ramatel pinched his eyes closed.

I never should have made her fight.

After several more hours, Asael seemed mostly healed. The large angel approached Ramatel who was still clutching Clara's body, and placed a hand on Ramatel's shoulder.

"I'm sorry, Brother." Asael sat down beside Ramatel, giving Ramatel a glimpse at the now unpierced and reformed face. No burn scars remained.

Ramatel glanced at his scarred forearms that held the body of his beloved, and felt a furious anger boiling to the top.

"Why Asael? Why'd he have to take her?"

"I don't know."

"Torture and scars weren't enough. I never should have come here. I never should have come back. I should have stayed in hell. She'd have been safe."

"No—" Asael started, but he didn't get to finish the sentence. Ramatel began to disappear.

"Fuck!" Asael screamed, drawing the attention of the one healer who was still awake and packing up. "Tell Gabriel he went up there!" Asael ordered, then disappeared himself.

Chapter Twenty Four

Asael blinked against the stark brilliant light he hadn't seen in thousands of years. The gate looked about the same as it ever had, but Asael didn't have time to take in the details. Ramatel was storming up to the gate with a vengeance.

"No Ramatel! Wait!"

Ramatel didn't slow, instead he thrust open the gate and dashed into the courtyard to the hall. Asael sprinted after him still limping a little from his previous injuries. Before Ramatel could gain any more ground, and Asael managed to tackle him to the ground.

"Get the fuck off me! What are you doing?"

"I'm stopping you from committing suicide!"

"It's not right! It's not right and He needs to hear it!" Ramatel bellowed, elbowing Asael in the side.

"I know man. I know."

"No, you *don't* know!" Ramatel cried back and wrestled Asael off. Ramatel ran head long for the hall. Just as Anachel stepped before him to block his path, Gabriel appeared on the steps and tackled Ramatel as Asael had done moments before, and Asael hurriedly ran to help.

"It's not fair! I love her! Let me up!" Ramatel cried between sobs.

Asael held tight to Ramatel's arm. "Not yet. We aren't going to let you in there like this."

"Arrrg!" Ramatel screamed into Gabriel's arm. "What if she is in there being judged right now? He needs to know that it was my idea for her to be there. He needs to know she was a good *chinfon*. He needs to know I love her! He needs to know—" his sobbing stopped him.

"*She...*" he sobbed, "She needs to know I love her," he choked out through tears.

***

There was a sense of peace that filled every part of Clara like she had never experienced before. A light, so bright that Clara couldn't even bear to squint at it, shone before her. She was in some kind of a hall, but not an earthly one. This was far too radiant and lovely to be a part of the same realm where evil is tolerated.

"CLARA, YOU COMPLETED YOUR TASK VERY QUICKLY," spoke a voice from the bright light. The power from the voice alone left her momentarily awestruck. The voice could only have come from God.

"I... um, I'm done?"

"YES YOU ARE. WOULD YOU LIKE TO KNOW WHAT YOUR CHALLENGE WAS?"

"Yes, um, Father?" she added the last bit tentatively, feeling rather unprepared. *What title am I supposed to use to address the Lord?*

"HERE, LET ME SHOW YOU SOMETHING."

Clara was struck with a vision in her mind, as though she was conjuring a memory that she was unaware she possessed. It was as if the memory was proceeding in fast forward. It was going so fast it didn't allow her time to catch details.

First, she was sworn in as some kind of law enforcement agent. She transferred units and was assigned to a task force. Then she was undercover at a drug exchange in a motorcycle gang. Then another. An execution. More executions of a rival gang. She saw herself kissing the gang leader. She didn't know how she knew he was the gang leader. She just did. There was emotion in that kiss. Passion.

Then came a raid from the police. There was decision to be made in a split second. She hesitated to fight the leader and a good officer had died. Then again, she saw that image of the muzzle flash that killed her. The emotional weight of that revelation dropped Clara to her knees.

Betrayal. Fear. Disappointment in herself. Grief for the fallen officer.

"He killed me," she whispered. "He killed the officer and me."

"YES. YOU WERE SUPPOSED TO BE UNDER COVER, BUT YOU WENT TOO FAR UNDER. YOU COULD HAVE FOUGHT TO SAVE THAT OFFICER, BUT YOUR FEAR, AND YOUR FEELINGS, HELD YOU BACK."

Grief and guilt pounded together into her heart. "I'm so sorry."

"THAT WAS NOT THE CASE THIS TIME CLARA. YOU HAVE REDEEMED YOURSELF. YOU DIED IN A FIGHT AGAINST THE DEMONS."

He doesn't know about the command? Should I tell him? Will that damn me? Do I really want to spend eternity living a lie?

"Father, I couldn't do that. My *chinshen* commanded me into that battle."

"NO CLARA, HE DID NOT. YOU WERE UNDER NO ONE'S WILL BUT YOUR OWN. IN FACT…" The voice sounded amused. "HE IS OUTSIDE THE DOOR THROWING A TANTRUM AS WE SPEAK. IT SEEMS

HE HAS COME TO CHALLENGE ME, BEG FOR
LENIENCY, BEG FOR YOU TO BE RETURNED, AND
DEMAND AN AUDIENCE WITH YOU. ALL AT
ONCE, I SUPPOSE. HE IS VERY CONFUSED
TODAY." A powerful deep chuckle sounded throughout
the hall. "HE HAS TWICE THREATENED TO KILL
ME, AND SEVERAL TIMES OFFERED TO TRADE
HIS SOUL FOR YOURS. HE EVEN OFFERED TO
RETURN TO THE ABYSS IN EXCHANGE FOR YOUR
PLACE HERE."

Clara felt a panic. Ramatel had threatened to kill the
Father?! Is that even possible? "Please forgive him Father,
he is distraught! Ang please don't send him back to the
abyss! "

"YES, I KNOW. EASE YOUR MIND, I'D NOT
SEND HIM BACK FOR THIS. TELL ME CLARA,
WOULD YOU RETURN TO HIM IF YOU HAD THE
CHANCE?"

Clara wanted to hope that was possible, but she
couldn't bring herself to set herself up for that degree of
disappointment. No one ever came back from the dead.
What could being honest hurt now though?

"Yes, I would Father. For all his faults, I love him
anyway."

It felt like the bright being grinned, but since she
couldn't see it, she had no idea what gave her that
impression. "WOULD YOU CARE TO JOIN THE
ANGEL RANKS OF EARTH THEN? IT WOULD
MEAN PUTTING OFF YOUR STAY HERE, AND
POSSIBLY EVEN JEOPARDIZING IT, SHOULD YOU
SUCCUMB THE TEMPTATIONS OF EVIL."

Clara tried to look up and was instantly reminded by the brightness of why she was looking down in the first place. The serenity and joy of this place was excruciatingly tempting, but the memory of the look in Ramatel's eyes as he'd stared down at her made up her mind. That, she decided, was heaven for her.

"Yes please, Father. I would."

"THEN GO AND JOIN HIM..." There was a thoughtful pause. ".. AND TELL RAMATEL THAT HE NEED NOT BREAK HIS VOW TODAY IF HE DOES NOT WANT TO."

Clara felt herself leap, literally and emotionally. She turned and began to leave, but she was reminded of something. *Should I ask? If I don't I may not get another chance.*

"Father?"

"YES CHILD."

"I would like to ask permission for Ramatel and I to enter a romantic relationship."

"THAT IS BETWEEN YOU AND HIM. MY ANGELS MAY CHOOSE THEIR OWN RELATIONSHIPS."

A wide beaming grin overtook Clara's face. "Thank you Father!" Clara crossed the distance between her and the ornate doors at the far end of the hall, where she could still hear Ramatel screaming, as fast as her legs could carry her. With a push on the door that led her out into a courtyard, she was greeted by a beautiful female angel holding a staff. Just beyond the beautiful angel Ramatel was being held down by Asael, who was no longer pierced, and Gabriel.

"Ramatel!" Clara cried, as she dove for the mass of male angels wrestling on the ground. She pushed them off Ramatel throwing her arms around his neck. Ramatel's eyes widened and his face lit up when saw her. His strong arms clasped her to his chest, rendering her immobile.

"Clara!?" He kissed her and pulled away. "Clara is that really you?"

"It's me Ramatel. I'm here." More kissing.

"Clara, I'm so sorry. I should have protected y—" she covered his mouth with hers, cutting off whatever he was going to say. When they managed to separate, Ramatel put both of his hands on Clara's face and held her. "Clara, I love you."

"I love you too, Ramatel. You saved me." Tears formed at the corners of her eyes. "Take me home."

"No, I-"

"You saved me," she interjected. "If you had commanded me, I wouldn't have passed the judgement." She pressed her lips against his again, and felt the wetness of their tears on her cheek.

Chapter Twenty Five

A warm reception from the entire house greeted Clara when she returned and told them the story of what happened. There were strong embraces from everyone and even tears from Jahi. The grand dining room was still in complete disarray, and the people were each in various stages of dress and cleanliness. Many still were wearing goo-covered fighting attire. Some had showered and changed. Amy was hard at work cleaning Clara's blood off the tile. What had felt like only moments to Clara, had apparently been an entire night now down here.

One healer remained and seemed relieved to see that Clara had come back. *I wonder what that was about.* For some reason, Ramatel apologized to her. The healer insisted on looking over Asael before she left, despite his insistence that he was fine.

The babies were now all swaddled and sleeping, with Liwet rocking one of them and Sarah on a glider. He'd tried to get up to embrace Clara, but she held out a hand to stop him and gave him a peck on the cheek instead. Such a strange sight to see this large, ripped warrior with a baby in each arm, gliding back and forth on a flowered cushion.

Zachriel had gone to mind swipe the women and release them at a police station with a new story about an all night rave that got out of hand. Alex was still at the cage helping Zachriel. Hamal and Butator embraced Clara and welcomed her into their ranks. Barakel, Maria, Julie, Brian, and Jeffrey would be told when they woke up. Gabriel thought it best to let them sleep for now. Barakel had expended a lot of himself with the lightning and, apparently, all but collapsed upon returning home.

Ramatel followed a step behind Clara everywhere she went as she reunited with everyone. He refused to let go of her for even a second, touching some part of her at all times. Holding her hand, the small of her back, anything. Finally, Clara had greeted everyone and wanted some long awaited alone time with Ramatel, so they headed back to their room.

They'd just closed the door behind them when Ramatel pulled Clara into his chest and nuzzled her neck. "I love you," he whispered into her ear. "I need you to know that."

She wrapped her arms around his giant solid torso. "I do. I love you too." They held each other for a moment, relishing the feel of the embrace. Clara broke the silence. "The father had a message for you." She felt Ramatel's body stiffen immediately. "He said you don't have to break your vow today if you don't want to." The tension eased and Ramatel breathed a sigh of relief, so Clara continued. "He also told me that angels can choose their own relationships."

This brought a smile to his face, one of those rare genuine smiles that teased her own lips to curl up. Ramatel stepped back and took a knee on the floor. He reached for Clara's hand.

"I don't have ring like the humans use, but I'll get one. Clara will you choose me?"

Her grin broadened and she dragged him off the floor. "I choose you!" They held each other for a long moment and kissed until their lips were swollen. Clara felt him stiffen against her but he didn't move. She was beginning to wonder if they were going to do this all day, so she started to inch him further into the room, but he pulled her back. His adam's apple bounced like he was swallowing.

He was nervous.

***

"C'mon," she said, tenderly pulling him toward the bathroom. "Let's get cleaned up. You still have…um… that," she pointed to the demon blood on his shirt.

Embarrassment flooded his cheeks and Ramatel lightly slapped his hand to his face then raked his hand down down. "I can't believe I went up there with demon blood on me," he whispered, horrified. "We all did, didn't we?" When Clara nodded Ramatel shook his head. "Oh man…"

"C'mon." She tugged on his arm and he followed her.

They stripped in the bathroom and waited for the water to heat. Ramatel felt himself harden at the sight of her naked in front of him. Her lush pale skin bared for him, those perky sensuous breasts and puckered pink nipples made him groan but he knew he had to hold back. At least until the evil residue was off him. He didn't want a drop of that touching her pale skin.

There was more to the waiting though. His stomach was fluttering like he was a high school quarterback about to lose his virginity. It was the real deal this time. The beginning of forever. He had to make it good. The last time they were together she was so drugged and aroused that a strong breeze would have sent her over the edge.

This time, it was just him. Just him and seventy generations without practice. *Can I even do this?*

She stepped into the shower and he followed behind her with his eyes glued to her tight ass. He wasn't even going to let a shower curtain separate them, not after losing her once already. Before she could get her arms around him again he'd soaped up. Not that he didn't want her arms around him, he just couldn't stand the thought of her being contaminated by that black blood.

Yeah, that was it. He wasn't stalling.

When he had scrubbed sufficiently, they swapped places and he stepped under the spray to rinse off. The warm water hit his eyes, causing them to close, only to fly open at the feeling of her hand caressing its way across his stomach, then lower. His cock jerked as if it knew what was coming.

"Clara—" he started, but was cut off by her lips pressing into his. He wanted to deepen the kiss but doubt held him back.

She must have noticed. "What is it?" Those gorgeous green eyes fixed on him.

"It's just that I... uh... it's been a long time for me—"

She pressed a finger to his lips, steadying them. "Ssshh. Ramatel, I love you. I know what you are capable of. You have nothing to worry about."

His eyes wrinkled into a smile and he pulled her into his body, causing her to push her breasts into him. A surge of lust shot through his body and he couldn't resist the urge to cup one of her lush mounds. Her nipples were taught already and he ran his thumb back and forth over it, causing a moan to escape her lips. He looked down at his scarred hand touching her flawless cleansed skin. A part of him still couldn't believe she was here.

She was alive. Here. With him. She loved him.

He turned the water off with his mind and scooped her up into his arms.

She made a sound of surprise then giggled. Without bothering to towel her dry he carried her to the bed, their bed, and gently laid her down. She reached for him and drew him to her, sucking his tongue into her mouth. This kiss was soft, slow, and endearing.

"I love your taste," he breathed in her lips. Then he pulled away, eliciting a whimper as he did. "I'm going to taste you again," he promised, shifting his position and crawling between her welcoming legs.

Ramatel dipped his mouth until he could smell her aroma, the pleasing musk that was the most glorious scent in the world. He tasted the edge of her folds, sliding up and down, before prodding them to part with his tongue. Her fingers entwined themselves in his wet hair and he looked up at her. Her green eyes were half shrouded with eyelashes and her mouth was parted, lips still swollen from kissing.

Just as these would soon be. He lapped at her entrance and her hips bucked toward his mouth. He continued to lick at her sex until she was panting and arching her back. Then he adjusted his position and slowly caressed her sensitive nub until she was squirming.

"Ramatel," she begged in a husky voice. "Please."

He smiled, feeling his confidence return with each panting breath she took. He drew her into his mouth and ran his tongue over her in short rocking swirls until she screamed and clenched her legs tight around his neck. He eased back, but didn't stop his slow, easy suckle until she lay motionless on the bed with her eyes shut and a contented look on her face.

He climbed over her to see that look. That was the look he wanted her to wear for all time. She was breathing heavy but she still smiled, and eventually opened her eyes. He dipped his head again.

***

Clara felt both satiated and unfulfilled at the same time. He'd just given her a mind blowing orgasm but she wanted more. She wanted him, all of him.

Just as she'd had that thought, she felt him duck his head. A lap of folds sent a wave of sensation through her body. He didn't retract his tongue, rather he stroked the outside of her entrance until she was bucking her hips against him.

His shoulder had her legs spread wide and she felt both exposed and entranced. With each lick he promised more until her muscles contracted and her back was arched off the bed. An aching need pushed her to move, but he held her fast against the bed.

Finally, she felt the delicate probe of a wandering finger and she tried to push against it. Ramatel slid his finger easily inside her and began to piston it back and forth. A wonderful tension threatened to rip her apart from the inside if she wasn't filled soon and she thrust herself against his finger.

With a sudden move, his lips closed over her clitoris and Ramatel drew her into his mouth again while she skewered herself against his finger. Finally unable to resist for any longer, the immediate sensation drove her over the edge with a scream that was much louder than she intended.

Chapter Twenty Six

Ramatel watched her come again from his vantage point between her legs. He felt a surge of triumph and power that he'd brought her to release. She reached for him and pulled him closer, drawing him up to her face and encasing his body with her legs. He'd dreamt of this moment for so long, and now that it was here, he realized that she was better than he could have hoped.

Courageous. Strong. Gentle. Loving.

He positioned his cock at her drenched sex just as she kissed him, making little mewing noises that increased as he pressed himself slowly into her and then stilled. He pulled his mouth back to see those bright green eyes on him.

His.

He pressed more and felt himself moan at how warm and tight she was. Silky smooth and inviting. So warm. He withdrew a little and pushed back into her and she bucked her hips against him, teasing a smile from his lips. His body wanted him to plow in and ease her, but his mind told him to savor the moment, so he continued with his slow gentle rocking.

Her pretty pink lips were parted with ecstasy and her eyes told him that she was right there with him. He thrust into her more and her hips rose to meet his thrusts. He wondered how he had managed to deny himself this pleasure for so long. He felt her breasts push against his chest and he bowed his head to suckle at them. The cute little noises she was making urged him to continue. Her tight sheath sent jolts of pleasure through him at every pull and thrust.

He could tell her resistance was waning and he didn't want her to hold out. He leaned back and pulled her hips upward toward him and quickened his pace. Wetting his thumb with his mouth, he felt his way down to her swollen, sensitive nub and stroked over it with a pace that matched his thrusts. It only took a moment before he felt her muscles tense and her sheath squeeze. Her sex gripped him, squeezing throughout and he almost lost it.

Her back arched off the bed and a loud moan was pulled from her throat. Ramatel stilled himself and watched her orgasm. She was beautiful. She was his.

Pride swelled his chest. He'd given her this, and he intended to do again. Her breathing slowed and he watched her mind return to earth. The feeling of her wrapped around him was too enjoyable for him to move.

When she seemed fully restored he resumed his thrusting again, loving how sensitivity made her so responsive to every tiny little motion.

"Ramatel," she whispered hoarsely into his ear. "It's your turn. I want you to come."

He chuckled and turned his head to suckle her earlobe. "Did you forget?" She faced him with a confused look and he smiled. "I'm the angel of endurance."

Epilogue

The exhaustion hadn't dissipated with sleep for Gabriel, but he had to get up. There would still be a lot to do, though at least there would be many to help. His home was finally filled with life again. That thought made him smile until his mind wandered back to the remaining tasks.

The babies had to be delivered to the Carmelite Sisters, who were creating an orphanage just for them since the babies' families had been killed. Luckily the paperwork would go through miraculously fast, thanks to Butator's doctoring and Zachriel's persuasion. There were also general logistics that would have to be handled. Their weapons would need to be cleaned, sharpened, and re-infused. Asael would take care of that. He'd need to check on Barakel and maybe send him to a healer. Someone should make sure the human women made it home safely. The list continued to grow in his head.

Gabriel stretched and got out of bed. His body still felt heavy, but he could manage. Most in the house weren't up yet, but some of the staff would be. He dressed and descended the stairs to find the other angels. They'd all heard about Clara's rejuvenation already. Rather than sitting at the table, Gabriel leaned against the counter sipping coffee while his mind sifted and ordered the upcoming tasks. He'd given everyone several days off. They all could use some down time.

"Hey," Liwet interrupted his thoughts. The big man entered the kitchen in pajama bottoms and a t-shirt. Gabriel was surprised to see him up already, but the bloodshot eyes suggested that he hadn't slept at all.

"Morning."

"Can we talk?"

Gabriel nodded and led Liwet to the now empty dining room. Gabriel had a feeling he knew what it was about. He mentally kicked himself for not separating the angel and the baby sooner.

"I can't give her up," Liwet declared. "I'll give up fighting if I have to, but I can't give her up."

"Liwet," Gabriel started gently, "human babies need human parents. She can't stay here. We have to remain hidden. What are we going to do when she goes to school and says 'My daddy can fly?'"

Liwet's hurt and desperation seeped through the room. "I'll give up my wings. We'll live as humans."

Gabriel pinched his lips together. "You would be a target and so would she. She especially because she is human and weaker."

"I can home school her. We can hide."

"Yeah, because humans do so well being raised in isolation," he said sarcastically.

"Please Gabriel. I can't lose her."

Gabriel studied the angeling's pained expression and felt an old wound tear back open in his own heart. He should force them apart, it would be for their own good. They'd both be better off... and Liwet would never forgive him. It was that kind of hurt that turned angels against their kind.

The pain in his chest reminded Gabriel of another pain, more distant but just as sharp. It felt like the pain he had when he hadn't been able to stop those bombs. Just like he wouldn't be able to stop this disaster. Could he do it again? Could he cause that kind of pain to another? He knew the answer.

Gabriel put his cup on the counter. "We need to seek counsel from a higher authority. Come with me." They disappeared.

***

"Stop, that tickles!" Clara exclaimed feeling Ramatel lightly rub the back of his hand against her stark white wings. She was trying to move a pencil with her mind but failing at anything other than staring at the pencil and giving herself a headache. How would she ever be able to teleport herself if she couldn't even move a pencil? Her wings had been sprouting from her back whenever she had an intense emotion, like the furious frustration she was feeling now. Ramatel said that was a survival instinct, but it only made her more frustrated.

"I can't help it. They're so new, and soft," he gave one of her wings another gentle pet.

"What if they do this at the party?"

"Well I hope you'll be having fun and not this frustrated." He bent down to kiss the top of her head. "Unless you want to sneak off and do something exciting," he added with a devilish look.

"We won't be able to. Jahi might need us." The fallen had warned Jahi about what the other angels would probably think about her, but she'd insisted that they would come to like her if they spent some time with her. Ramatel had expressed his doubts on the matter, enough so that the invitations were sent out under Gabriel's and Michael's names.

Clara saw Ramatel grimace at the reminder. "Yeah. True." His eyes met hers in the mirror ahead of them. "Guess we'll just have to compensate now."

"Are you trying to kill me?" Clara asked even though she smiled and turned to wrap her arms around his neck.

He still shot her a guilty look. "Too much?" They'd basically spent the last three days in bed, not sleeping.

Her lips pressed against his. "Never." She pushed him backward until his knees hit the bed and forced him to sit, then she knelt between his legs. His cock jerked to life in anticipation.

Soon after they lay on the bed entwined in each other's arms. Clara's lips felt swollen and she was happy for the reprieve from the staring contest with the pencil. Ramatel's arms were wrapped around her, his fingers lazily caressing her skin.

"C'mon," she sat up. "We need to get ready for this party. I promised Maria I'd help in the kitchen." He groaned in protest but forced his body off the bed. "This is going to be a disaster."

"What is?"

"All of us, all of them, the baby-"

"What about the baby?" Clara interrupted.

"They won't like that a newbie got to keep a baby."

Clara rolled her eyes. "Are angels always this jealous?"

Ramatel snickered. "Jealous, vain, whiny, you name it. We have the same emotions as the humans."

"Petty," she added. Clara got up and pushed the pencil with her finger just to give herself the satisfaction of having made it move somehow.

"Exactly, see this is a bad idea," Ramatel began to dress himself in his usual t-shirt style, but kept the jeans rather than the heavy cargo pants.

"Maybe some fun is what they need. They seemed really serious before. It might be good for them to mingle with you guys so they can see that you're still an angel."

Ramatel pinched his lips. "Debatable," he mumbled.

Hours later Clara, Ramatel, and Barakel waited in the living room of their small house. They'd dressed for the party, Clara in a cocktail dress, and the men in black button down shirts and jeans.

"You look hot in that," Clara whispered into Ramatel's ear and his eyes lit up.

Their moment was interrupted by Barakel bellowing to Asael. "Hurry that shit up, Ass. The only one you're going home tonight with is me and you aren't my type."

Asael emerged with his eyeliner heavy and his skin re-pierced. "You're just scared you can't handle the viper."

"Pssht, more like earthworm."

Asael grabbed his crotch. "I got your earthworm right here bro, and it would tear you in half."

"Let's go fellas," Clara cut in knowing that shit talking would go on forever, literally.

It was already dark out. Clara had been back inside their house for several hours after helping with the food, so the sight the few cars visible from their vantage point drew her attention. She smiled when she realized that the cars for the *chinfon* of the angels who couldn't transport their help themselves.

The sound of loud music coming from the dining room hit their ears as soon as they opened the back door to the house. Clara led them into the dining room that now contained a buffet style appetizer spread, a dance floor at the opposite end where Butator had set up Jahi's music, and several groups of beautiful mingling angels.

Some of the angels Clara recognized from the fight, some she didn't. She heard Asael give one a smiling greeting as he moved in front of her to grasp the shoulders of a large man. He sat in a group of rugged looking angels sitting on padded benches in the corner, as far from the gloriously manicured angels as possible.

"Brother!" Asael pulled at the angel. "How the hell are you?"

The tall brunette gave a half-grin. "How the hell indeed." He returned the hug. "What happened to your face? Lose a bet?"

Ramatel sidled up to the crowd with Clara and embraced the newcomers as well, ensuring to introduce her as his wife to each of them in turn. She quickly pieced together that these were some of the other fallen, which explained the distance from the rest of the angels. They all either had dark or colored eyes, not the golden eyes of the untainted. Some had visible scars, but most had the hardened look of those who've seen too much. Some had unkempt hair, others wore facial hair like Barakel, though it did not seem like any of these others took it as far as Asael with his make-up and piercings.

Clara glanced around the room, taking in the perfectly built, groomed, flawless angels on the other side of the room. She waved at Zachriel and Alex, and spotted Jahi on Michael's arm. Jahi was wearing a mini black

dress and leopard print, four inch, stilettos. She was
smiling, but Clara could tell it was fake. Her smiled didn't
reach her eyes.

Clara watched as Michael introduced her to
everyone and the newcomers grinned politely while
Michael was looking, but whispered through glares as
soon as Michael and Jahi walked away. *Poor thing.* Clara
excused herself and went to join Jahi.

"Jahi!" Clara called, practically wrestling the former
demon off Michael's arm, and pulling her into a dramatic
embrace for all others to see. "Come with me, I need to
show you something." Clara led Jahi out of the room to the
adjacent billiards room in the same way Jahi had once led
Clara through the club.

"You ok?" Clara asked once they were in the bar
room.

"No," Jahi sniffed, on the verge of tears. "They hate
me. I can hear what they say about me."

"They're stuck up snobs. Why do you care what
they think?"

"They're Michael's people," she sniffled. "He likes
them." Sniffle. "But all they care about is that I'm a demon
prostitute."

"No, you're Michael's wife. He might like them, but
he loves you. Did you see the way he introduced you to
everyone? He's proud of you. He'd walk through hell or
high water for you."

Jahi smiled a little and dabbed at her eyes. "He
already has."

Clara grinned. "My point exactly."

Jahi took a deep breath to center herself then pulled
out a makeup compact from her cleavage, making Clara

wonder how she'd been hiding it there in the first place, and proceeded to touch up her face. "Thanks Clara. Let's get back in there."

The first hour of the party was a lesson in awkwardness with the fallen on one side of the room, the gorgeous on the other, the angelings mostly keeping to themselves, and the chinfons mingling about with each other. Occasionally a few of the glorious angels would venture over to the fallen's side of the table to greet Clara and welcome her, usually escorted by Zachriel, Michael, or Gabriel, as if they needed an escort to venture into a lion's den.

Michael seemed oblivious to Jahi's cold reception by the other angels but he continued to dote on her incessantly as only he could. Gabriel mingled among the guests, trying to ensure others were having a good time, but the crease in forehead was an ever present reminder of that his thoughts were elsewhere.

As soon as they'd publicly presented Sarah and welcomed her to the family, the official reason for the party, Asael led the fallen to the billiards room that they occupied for the rest of the night, preferring to keep to themselves with the hard liquor and pool table. Once divided, both parties seemed much more at ease. The volume of conversation in the dining room rose. Clara saw cheers and toasts called over the heads of the now laughing glorious angels whenever she went to check on Jahi.

The fallen were a somber bunch, and most of the conversation was shit talking to each other. The level of aggression in this room was far higher, instead of toasts and cheers, punches and insults were exchanged, usually in jest - but some were questionable. They seemed to feel at home among each other, although they welcomed Clara with open arms.

"Fuck!" Asael bellowed, having missed a shot on the pool table.

"Trouble getting it in the hole?" Michael called, walking in with Jahi and the healer that had tended to Asael the night of the fight.

"I must be out of practice. Why don't you come over here and bend over?" Asael fired back then winked to the healer whose face immediately turned deep red.

Michael just chuckled and shook his head. Clara sensed that Asael was going to go into 'offending' mode so she joined the two women at the bar where Jahi was pouring drinks.

"How's it going out there?" Clara asked.

"Actually pretty good now, but all they have to drink in that room is wine," Jahi complained, handing the healer a cup of something green. "Try this, it's sweet. You'll like it I promise."

The healer took the glass and tentatively sipped it. A warm smile spread across her face when she swallowed the mixture. "That is good!" she pronounced with a grin.

Clara smiled back, happy that some of the snobby crowd were warming to Jahi. Clara hadn't noticed Asael follow her to the bar, but she saw him lean down to the healer. "If you wanted something sweet in your mouth, all you had to do was ask honey."

The woman's mouth dropped in horror, and even Jahi turned red.

"Asael!" Clara yelled, and hit him in the arm at the same time. She gave him her most pissed off look and leaned toward him. "Don't ruin this for Jahi," Clara hissed into his ear. "She is making friends."

Asael shot Jahi an apologetic look but he pointed avoided looking at the healer. "I was just being friendly," he replied coldly then returned to his game. Clara suspected he was being territorial and trying to run the glorious angel out of the billiards room and back to the other side of the party.

"Hey Jahi," Michael cut in, but his eyes were on Gabriel's tense body in the doorway to the dining room. "Something is missing. I'll be right back. Can you make sure Gabriel doesn't go anywhere?"

Jahi gave him a curious look but nodded, and Michael disappeared from view. Jahi and the healer returned to the dining room with their green drinks and Clara trailing after them, still feeling like she had to apologize for Asael.

***

Michael emerged minutes later from the direction of the living room, followed by a stunningly beautiful angel that Clara recognized from the hall in heaven. She had a long dark hair, a round face, and large doe-like eyes. The angels all seem to leap up in exuberance as she entered behind Michael, still in the traditional garb of heaven.

"Anachel," Gabriel gave a wondrous shake of his head as if he couldn't believe his eyes. He was at her side in an instant, pulling her into an embrace. Others it seemed had the same idea, but they had to wait their turn.

"She hasn't been back to earth in a long time," the healer, who had introduced herself as Isda, explained. "I'm going to greet her."

Clara watched the procession as Anachel greeted everyone with bright smiles and warm hugs, wondering if she was expected to join into this reception gauntlet. Even the fallen had emerged from their man cave to see what the fuss was about. Some had turned to go back, when an unexpected silence filled the hall.

Michael was at the DJ table, maneuvering something behind speakers. The sound of soft stringed instruments began to weave itself into the ears of those in the hall. Blank stares changed to recognizing smiles on some of the presumably older angels, including Anachel. It didn't sound like a guitar, but perhaps something similar, but older. A drum beat began soon followed by the soft but quick melody of a violin cutting through the base of the guitar-like instrument.

It may have been a celtic jig or some medieval dancing song. The music grew louder and the beat of the drum was picked up by some of the angels gathering around the edge of the dance floor who clapped their hands and stopped their feet in time to the music.

Jahi was beaming at Michael and she met him on the dance floor. Zachriel had found a light haired woman in a green dress to dance with, and Gabriel was escorting Anachel toward the empty space. Others Clara didn't know joined them, and the beat of the clapping hands and stomping feet reverberated throughout the room filling it with an exciting anticipation.

The men formed a line on one side, their dancing partners on the other. Some silent cue triggered a move toward each other. The dancing angels began to twirl around each other in time to the music.

Hands touched, then bodies.

They stepped away from each other, then back in. They moved as if choreographed, men lifting the women, women stepping back then forward, both clapping to each other at certain times. Feet quickly stepping in time with each other and the clapping.

As the music picked up in volume and energy, the dancing angels, and Jahi, freed their wings, making the dance floor look a mass of feathery swirls, all white save for Jahi's dark gray. Michael maneuvered her to the center so it looked like an intentional design. Wings met wings, hands clapped, and feet bounced.

Even the fallen remained in the dining room to see the show as the partners circled each other in a quick pace. Everyone in the room smiled on, watching the few ancient angels that knew this dance. Clara felt Ramatel's arms circle her waist, and she looked away from the show long enough to brush her lips against his neck.

It was hard to miss the way Anachel and Gabriel smiled at each other as if the other was the only other being on the Earth. Clara had never seen him so carefree, so… happy.

There was a contagious glimmer in Anachel's eyes that dared everyone to try to be anything but happy in front of her. There was something else too, something in the way she and Gabriel moved together, an energy between them. Clara glanced around to see if she was the only one who noticed. All eyes were locked on the couple moving across the dance floor as if they shared one soul.

"Why aren't they together?" Clara whispered to Ramatel who was also studying the couple.

"I don't know," he whispered back. "They must not know what they are missing." He pressed his lips to her cheeks and pulled her tighter.

Like the book? Leave a review!

Watch for the next book in A Series of Angels, and follow me!

Facebook

https://www.facebook.com/AuthorJoelCrofoot

Twitter

https://twitter.com/JoelWCrofoot

Amazon

https://www.amazon.com/Joel-Crofoot/e/B01LVX8KC7

About the Author

I was raised in northern New York State on a farm. At 18 years-old I enlisted in the Marine Corps and spent my first 4 years in Japan working as a radio operator. I then became a bomb disposal technician (it's called explosive ordnance disposal) and returned to the U.S. to be stationed out of California. I did 2 combat tours to Iraq then left the Marine Corps to pursue higher education. I currently reside in Los Angeles and anticipate graduating with a doctorate in psychology in the fall of 2017. In my free time I enjoy running, playing with my dogs, and reading.

19281576R00108

Printed in Great Britain
by Amazon